Little Ed

Ed Englefield, editor of the *Baker Street Bugle* school magazine, is in trouble. Issue No. 17 has only sold eleven copies, and if No. 18 doesn't do a lot better, the *Bugle* will have to go. So Ed sets off on a hunt for a Searing Human Drama to boost sales, and on the way meets up with a glamorous film star, a temperamental footballer and a large and affectionate dog called Charlesworthy Sunnysides Badminton the Fourth.

Tom Tully is well known as a writer of sports stories and picture stories, and is the author of Roy of the Rovers. He is also the author of *The Beaver Book of Football* and *Football Quiz*, both published by Beaver.

Little Ed

Tom Tully

Illustrated by Lesley Smith

Beaver Books

First published in 1979 by
Frederick Warne (Publishers) Limited
40 Bedford Square
London WC1B 3HE

This paperback edition published in 1980 by
The Hamlyn Publishing Group Limited
London · New York · Sydney · Toronto
Astronaut House, Feltham, Middlesex, England
(Paperback Division: Hamlyn Paperbacks
Banda House, Cambridge Grove
Hammersmith, London W6 0LE)

© Copyright Text Tom Tully 1979
© Copyright Illustrations
Frederick Warne (Publishers) Limited 1979
ISBN 0 600 20120 1

Set, printed and bound in Great Britain by
Cox and Wyman Limited, Reading
Set in Intertype Garamond

Contents

A bad day for the Bugle

Edward Englefield watched the last, chattering group of children straggle out through the school gates, and resigned himself to the fact that he wasn't going to sell any more copies of the school magazine. Not as far as Issue No. 17 was concerned, anyway. Out of the fifty copies he had printed the previous evening, only eleven had been actually purchased by the boys and girls of Baker Street School. Two more had been pinched by some Third Year hooligans, and Johnny Rackham had cadged a free copy, in return for the promise of an exclusive interview with Johnny's older brother, who played for Chiverton Athletic reserves.

Shifting his weight from one foot to the other, Ed came to the conclusion that it wasn't much fun being the youngest magazine editor in the world if hardly anyone wanted to buy your product ... It was such good value, too, even if it *was* printed on blue rough-paper and the pages bound together with Sellotape.

As he began to gather up the unsold magazines from the small folding table that stood against the wall, Ed wondered if he ought to scrap the Jokes Page, and try a few Horoscopes. All that stuff about stars and lucky

omens would certainly appeal to the senior girls. His mind toyed some possible headlines. 'CONSULT THE ZODIAC WITH ED' ... or 'CAPRICORNIANS TAKING EXAMS THIS MONTH CAN EXPECT FAVOURABLE RESULTS'. Yes, that wasn't bad. Why on earth hadn't he thought of it before?

Tucking the table under one arm, and unsold magazines under the other, Ed set off across the deserted playground. 'MONEY SIGNS LOOK GOOD, WITH THE CHANCE OF AN INCREASE IN POCKET-MONEY ON TUESDAY,' he said aloud, breaking into a trot. His earlier mood of depression had vanished, and now he couldn't wait to get back to the office, so that he could make a start on the new feature.

The 'office' where Ed produced the *Baker Street Bugle* once a month was actually a tiny, cluttered store-room adjoining the school gymnasium. Ed's battered duplicating machine occupied a corner by the window, and apart from a couple of shelves crammed with back-numbers of the *Bugle*, the only other item of furniture was a wooden trestle table. Strewn with stencilling sheets, pens, and bottles of printing ink, it stood trapped in a musty forest of long-forgotten sports equipment. Now, as Ed struggled through the door, he saw to his dismay that he had a visitor . . . in the bespectacled, beefy-necked form of Mr Gillard, the Assistant Headmaster.

'Well now, Englefield,' Mr Gillard began, eyeing the stack of unsold magazines still clutched under Ed's right arm. 'Business seems to have been a little slow today. How many copies of the *Bugle* have you sold?'

'I . . . er . . . haven't checked up yet, sir, but I should think it's quite a few.'

'How many, Englefield?'

'I should do a bit better tomorrow, sir. There were a lot of kids away on a field exercise, y'see.'

'I ASKED YOU HOW MANY!'

'Eleven, sir.'

Ed found himself holding his breath as Mr Gillard frowned, shook his head, and adjusted his glasses. 'Now let me see . . . at two pence per copy, that means you've taken the princely sum of twenty-two pence. Not good enough, my lad. You haven't even covered the cost of your printing ink.'

'I haven't been round the staff yet, sir,' Ed said hastily. 'Will you be taking your usual copy?'

'I'm not sure, Englefield. To be quite frank, I am not entirely convinced that the *Bugle* is worthy of my continued support.'

For an instant, Mr Gillard's moist eyes roved over the small, untidy figure before him. There were smudges of ink on Ed's round, anxious face, and even a streak or two in his mop of reddish hair. Pencils and felt-nibbed pens poked up from his shirt-pockets like little rows of coloured organ-pipes, and Ed's grey trousers sagged under the weight of the large notepad that he always carried, wedged under his belt. Mr Gillard shuddered inwardly. The boy wasn't so much untidy as . . . well . . . *shapeless.* He looked as if he had been dragged backwards through his own duplicating machine.

'I have been looking through this month's edition,' Mr Gillard went on, helping himself to a copy of the *Bugle*, 'and I think I can see why it isn't selling. There seems to be a general lack of . . .' Mr Gillard groped for the word he wanted '. . . EXCITEMENT! Yes, that's it. An absence of features that will fire the imagination.'

'The *Bugle* used to do all right before the Gossip Column was stopped, sir.'

'Now that was your own fault, Englefield. You shouldn't have published items of gossip about the staff. Not even the Headmaster was aware that Mrs Goodenough had been fined for speeding on her Yamaha.' Mr Gillard stabbed at one of the pages. 'And take this article about glass-blowing. It's hardly the kind of thing to stir the blood of a healthy, soccer-mad schoolboy, is it?'

'Mr Forbes wrote that article, sir. I think he does it as a sort of hobby.'

'What, article-writing?'

'No, glass-blowing. He says he's going to blow up a vase in our next science period, and—'

'All right, Englefield,' Mr Gillard cut in irritably. 'We're supposed to be discussing the contents of the *Bugle*, not what Mr Forbes does in his spare time.' He peered short-sightedly at another page, eyes widening in sudden interest. 'Now this analysis of the school dinners looks promising . . . but you can hardly read it. It seems to peter out at the Braised Liver and Chips.'

'That was the machine, sir,' Ed explained. Trust Mr Gillard to notice that smudgy page. 'I think it needs a new roller. Actually, I could do with a whole new machine,' he added hopefully.

'It's a poor workman who blames his own tools, Englefield.' Rubbing at his large lumpy nose, Mr Gillard began to pick his way around the table through the confusion of sports gear. 'No, my lad. As I pointed out just now, the *Bugle* suffers from a lack of drama and excitement. You should be concentrating on stories that reflect the triumphs and tragedies of ordinary people. The stuff of life, Englefield. In other words . . . HUMAN INTEREST!'

With an emphatic and commanding gesture that he often used in the classroom, Mr Gillard lifted his right hand, and brought it down hard on the trestle table. Unfortunately it landed in a pool of ink which Ed had spilt during afternoon break. Most of the ink sprayed on to the floor, but some of it squirted up Mr Gillard's arm. Several small black dots appeared on his glasses, as if by magic.

The Assistant Headmaster kept staring at Ed as if nothing unusual had happened. After a moment he said quietly, 'I'll give you until the next issue to improve the circulation, Englefield. Otherwise . . . the *Bugle* will have to go!'

Ed could hardly believe his ears. 'But, sir—'

'No "buts", young man.' Mr Gillard had found a scrap of blotting paper and was dabbing furiously at his inky palm. How, he asked himself, could one small child cause so much chaos, without even trying? Just wait until Mrs Gillard saw the stains on his shirt-sleeve. 'This room represents valuable storage space, and I cannot allow it to be wasted on an ailing publication.'

Ed couldn't think of anything to say as Mr Gillard lifted his ink-spotted glasses, located the door, and began to weave through the mass of equipment. 'But not to worry, Englefield. I am sure a determined young chap like you will soon dig up a "sensational scoop", as they say in the newspaper world. Why not start with your own family?' Mr Gillard's voice echoed down the corridor as he headed for the nearest cloakroom. 'Yes, that's it – the domestic ups-and-downs of the Englefields. *I'll bet there's a Searing Human Drama right under your own roof . . . !*'

Ed hardly heard the Assistant Headmaster's last impatient bellow of advice. At that particular moment the only Searing Drama on his mind was that the *Baker Street Bugle* seemed in danger of sounding the last post . . .

After clearing up the office as much as he could, Ed cycled homeward very slowly and very thoughtfully. Even though he had been expecting a few grumbles about the falling circulation of the *Bugle*, Mr Gillard's ultimatum had come as a shock. After all, he'd been doing his best. It wasn't easy to produce a decent magazine on a battered printing machine, with teachers insisting that he publish articles on weird subjects like glass-blowing.

Ed knew he wouldn't have such problems when he

grew up, and became the Editor of one of the big newspapers in London. Of course, he knew he would have to work up to it gradually, and become a reporter first. Ed had often imagined himself telephoning eye-witness reports from the trouble-spots of the world. Things like 'This is Edward Englefield, calling to you from the heart of this revolution-torn city. As I speak, bullets are whizzing around my ears, and a lump of plaster has just fallen on my typewriter . . .'

He had already sent an article entitled 'THE WORST EARTHQUAKES IN HISTORY' to the local newspaper, the *Chiverton Chronicle*, enclosing one of his home-made press cards, which read:

The article had been acknowledged by the Children's Features Editor, who had thanked Ed for his jolly story, and enclosed a green plastic badge, entitling him to a year's free membership of Uncle Ben's Corner. It wasn't quite the impact he had hoped to achieve, but there was plenty of time. The most important thing now was to save the *Bugle* – to dig up a 'scoop' that would send the circulation soaring.

When he arrived outside his home, Ed was reminded of Mr Gillard's last words 'I'll bet there's a searing drama, right under your very roof!' As he pushed his bike up the front path, past his father's prized magnolia tree, Number 19 Avon Close didn't look as if it was bursting at the seams with Searing Human Dramas. But he had to make a start somewhere, and you never knew with grown-ups.

Leaning his bike against the wall just outside the kitchen door, Ed began to prepare himself for the coming interviews. First, he opened his saddle-bag, and took out the old box camera which he had purchased at a scouts' jumble sale for twenty-five pence. Looping the camera-strap around his neck, Ed eased his notepad from under his belt, selected a red-ink biro, and checked that there were enough press cards in his right-hand shirt pocket. Then, taking a deep breath, he opened the kitchen door and peered in.

The kitchen was empty except for his mother, who, as usual, was trying to do several different things at the same time. He watched her zig-zagging back and forth through a faint, steamy haze for a second or two, and then said, as casually as he could, 'Hi, Mum! Can you er . . . spare a minute for a little chat?'

'Oh, not now, darling,' Mrs Englefield called breathlessly, charging over to the gas cooker. She bent to peer at something that was fizzing and crackling under the grill. 'Can't you see that I'm trying to get your father's dinner? I'm so far behind, it just isn't true!'

Mrs Englefield was always 'behind', or in a hurry. Sometimes, she whizzed around so fast, the rest of the family seemed to be standing still. Ed decided to press on while she was too busy to notice the state of his clothes. 'I was wondering if anything strange, or exciting had happened to you while you were out shopping today?'

'I'm sorry, Ed. You'll have to tell me about it later.'

'No, Mum ... I mean, did anything happen to *you*? Like being almost knocked down by a bus, or ... or the bread-men going on strike.'

'A BREAD-STRIKE?' Mrs Englefield skidded to a halt, and stared at Ed in horror. 'Oh, no ... not ANOTHER one! When's it going to start, Ed?'

'I dunno, Mum. I don't even know if there's going to BE one. I was only wondering—'

'Well, DON'T!' Mrs Englefield lunged at a saucepan of rice which was beginning to boil over. 'I'm behind enough as it is. I missed the bus back from your grandmother's, and I had to carry the baby all the way home. And apart from that, I promised to look in on Mrs Robinson. She's in hospital with ingrowing toenails.'

Ed's ears pricked up, and he took a firmer grip on his notepad.

'What's ingrowing toenails, Mum? Is it serious? Were you there when it happened?'

'Ingrowing toenails don't suddenly *happen*, you silly boy! Now for goodness' sake get out of my way, or—'

Mrs Englefield broke off as her eyes fell on a little trail of black, smudgy marks that Ed had left on her red-and-white tiled floor. 'Oh, no!' she screamed, wrenching open a cupboard, and pulling out a plastic bottle of scouring liquid. 'You little devil ... you've been standing in something! Just look at my clean tiles!'

More bottles and cartons of all shapes and sizes cascaded from the cupboard, as Mrs Englefield poured some cleaning fluid on to a rag, and began to scrub frantically at the dark, smudgy marks. 'The cleaner won't touch it. Oh, you clumsy little nuisance, Ed ... You must have trodden in some paint!'

Remembering the printing ink that Mr Gillard had splashed on to the office floor, Ed knew that it wasn't paint. But he had a feeling that this wasn't the time or place to say so.

'I'll have to use turpentine,' Mrs Englefield cried, scrambling to her feet and waving Ed towards the door. 'Go and fetch that bottle from the garden shed before the paint dries off!'

As Ed backed away he tripped over a stray carton, and lurched forward over the kitchen table. The sudden jolt was enough to send the contents of his shirt pockets showering over a large plate of half-made sandwiches. He just had time to retrieve most of his pens, pencils, erasers, and press cards, before a final shout of 'Get a move on, for goodness' sake. *And don't you dare come back in here with those shoes on!*' sent him stumbling out into the back garden.

Ed adjusted the strap of his camera, sighed wearily, and gazed at the words 'Ingrowing Toenails' which he had scribbled on the top sheet of his notepad. It didn't sound like the earth-shattering scoop that was going to save the *Bugle*. Perhaps, he told himself – catching sight of the lone figure that was toiling in the vegetable patch – he would have better luck with his father.

Mr Englefield was a tall, dark, impatient sort of man, who worked at a travel agency. His only ambition in life was to be left in peace to get on with his gardening – such as hoeing his autumn cabbages, of which Mr Englefield was particularly proud. He looked up sharply as Ed suddenly appeared through a screen of gooseberry bushes, and fixed suspicious eyes on the small, hopeful figure. Then, as if satisfied that he wasn't in any immediate danger, he carried on hoeing.

'Had a good day at school, son?' Mr Englefield said to the cabbages.

'Not too bad, Dad.' Ed had forgotten about the turpentine. Encouraged by the fact that his father seemed to have missed the commotion in the kitchen, he edged a little closer. 'Did *you* have a good day at work? I mean ... did anything sort of ... *exciting* happen to you?'

'No. Why should it have?'

'Oh, I was just wondering. I just thought that something dramatic might have happened ... like someone falling into the machinery, and having to be taken to hospital.'

'Well, I'm sorry to disappoint you, lad. We haven't got any machinery at the agency ... apart from a few typewriters, and a computer.'

'A computer?' Ed crossed out 'Ingrowing Toenails', and wrote down 'The Age of Computers'. This sounded promising. 'I didn't know you had a computer, Dad. Has it ever blown up, or anything like that?'

'Of course it hasn't,' his father snapped impatiently, his hoe stabbing at the weeds a little faster. 'It's just ... well ... gone wrong a couple of times, that all.'

'Has it really? And what happened when it went wrong, Dad?'

'A chap came round and put it right again. What on earth do you *think* happened?'

'Well, I thought you might have got all your bookings mixed up, and sent people off on holiday to the wrong places all over the world.'

'Now listen, son ... if you're going to keep on asking stupid questions like that—'

'*I* don't think they're stupid,' Ed went on doggedly. 'I mean, I heard of a computer once that kept on sending income tax demands to an alsatian.'

Mr Englefield opened his mouth as if to speak, clamped it shut again, and went on hoeing in utter silence. Ed was beginning to feel desperate.

'Surely *something* exciting must have happened to you at work today, Dad?'

'I'm warning you, Ed...'

'Maybe someone wanted their money back, because they had a rotten holiday? Maybe they came storming into your office, and—'

'All right, all right . . . I admit it!' Mr Englefield flung down his hoe and looked round at Ed, his eyes rolling wildly. 'I can't keep it to myself any longer. Something *did* happen at the office today – something *awful! A gang of escaped convicts stormed in, and took over the agency!*'

'CONVICTS?'

'Yes! There were six of 'em – ugly, unshaven brutes . . . armed to the teeth. They pointed a sawn-off shotgun at me, and demanded free air passage to Albania. But all we could offer them was four days on the French Riviera!' Mr Englefield was stamping up and down now, grimacing and grunting, and aiming punches at thin air. 'But they didn't frighten me, son. Oh, no! I just took a flying leap over the counter, and flattened their leader with a stack of brochures!'

'A stack of . . .? Aw, c'mon, Dad.' Ed suddenly realised that his father wasn't taking him seriously – that this strange display was actually a desperate attempt to discourage him from asking any more questions. He just stood and watched as Mr Englefield continued to leap about, and lash out at imaginary convicts.

'Two more went down under my pile-driving fists,' Mr Englefield gasped. 'But the others were closing in. One of them dived at my legs, and another jumped on my back! I felt his huge, hairy hands beginning to tighten around my throat! And then . . . *AAAAAOUGH!*'

Mr Englefield's last yell was quiet realistic. Which wasn't surprising because he had plonked a boot-shod foot on the prongs of his rake, which was lying nearby. As the handle shot up and cracked against the back of his head, Mr Englefield lost his balance, swayed like a wind-tossed oak tree, and fell face down on to the bed of cabbages.

For a wild moment Ed thought of taking a photograph of his sprawling parent, and entitling it 'Cabbages Crushed by Falling Travel Agent'.

But Mr Englefield was already swaying to his feet, gasping strange, uncompleted sentences such as 'Why, you stupid little ... You've gone and made me ...' Then he stepped on the rake again, and fell slowly backwards into a bed of onions, which he had just 'mulched' with well-rotted compost.

Ed had only a vague glimpse of this, for he was already half-way across the patio, and heading for the French windows. He had decided to make for his room by way of the lounge, thus by-passing the kitchen, where, no doubt, his mother was still scrubbing furiously at printing-ink stains.

As he reached the hall the front door burst open, and in flew his older sister, Karen. 'Ah-hah,' she yelled, grabbing Ed by the shoulders, and whirling him around. 'The Mighty Editor – just the chap I want to see. At precisely sixteen-thirty hours this afternoon, at the Baker Street School Swimming Baths, Miss Karen Elizabeth Englefield broke the Under-15 record for the eighty metres sprint!'

Karen beamed triumphantly, her shoulder-length hair still damp and glistening from the baths. 'There! How's that for a sensational story for the school magazine? I expect you'll want a detailed report ... photographs ...'

'Er, no thanks, Karen,' Ed edged towards the stairs, one ear cocked for the uproar that would undoubtedly erupt at any second. 'I'm afraid I've got enough material for next month's sports page.'

'Well, that's charming!' Karen snorted. 'You're always pestering me for an exclusive interview, and when I offer to give you a really fantastic one, you don't bloomin' well want it. Well, don't you ever ask me again, that's all!'

Pushing Ed aside, she flounced on into the kitchen. 'No wonder he can't sell his daft magazines. Mum, what's for tea? I'm starving. Have you got any sandwiches?'

Karen's last remark was almost drowned by the gale of noise that followed Ed up the stairs. Through a confusion of slamming doors, and overturning chairs, he heard his father yelling about crushed cabbages, and needing a bath . . . Then followed a sudden, spluttering scream from Karen. 'MY SANDWICH – IT'S FULL OF CARD-BOARD! I THINK I'VE SWALLOWED SOME OF IT!'

Trust a girl to make a fuss about a bit of cardboard, Ed thought, as he slipped into his room. He always printed his press cards on the cleanest cardoard he could find, so it wouldn't do her any harm. But that was typical of his family – always getting into a flap over nothing. He should have realised – despite Mr Gillard's advice – that nothing exciting *ever* happened under his own roof. He would have to search elsewhere for the Searing Human Drama that was going to save the *Bugle*.

As he sorted out a day-old copy of the *Chiverton Chronicle* from a pile of newspapers and magazines, Ed thought he heard his mother yelling something about turpentine. Then the muffled cries and rumblings from downstairs, merging with the howls of his baby brother in the next room, faded from his mind as he spread out the newspaper on his bed, and began to concentrate on the printed columns.

Ed was sure he had read an article about a famous film actress, who was coming to Chiverton for a few days, to shoot some scenes for her latest film. Yes . . . there it was.

Little Ed

Now if he could only get an exclusive interview with Miss Fiona Redburn ...

A taste of stardom

Ed was particularly pleased that the following day was Saturday. It was his father's busiest day at the travel agency, and Mr Englefield had already left for work by the time Ed crept downstairs. Karen was having her usual Saturday lie-in, and even his mother seemed to have calmed down a little. All she said was 'And what are YOU doing up so early?' before asking him to keep an eye on the Englefields' eighteen-month-old baby boy, while she organised something on the telephone.

Having just polished off a bowl of mashed cereal, and several toasty fingers, Joseph Mark Englefield – otherwise known as Baby Joe – hardly noticed his mother leaving the kitchen. He watched in fascinated silence from his high chair as Ed crept up to him like a furtive newspaper reporter, and hissed, 'Good morning, Miss Redburn. I'm Englefield from the *Bugle*. If you've no objections, I'd like to ask you for a few questions before you start the next scene.'

'Rrrrr!' beamed Baby Joe, not objecting in the least.

'Thank you, Miss Redburn. Now you must have played opposite loads of famous leading men during your amazing career. Which of them do you reckon was the most handsome?'

'Dad-Dad!'

'Really?' Ed made an imaginary note on his pad.
'That's very interesting. You played opposite him in *Gun-
smoke and Lollipops,* didn't you? Or was it *Love on a
Luncheon Voucher?*'

'AYBIE-JUR POO-POO!' squealed 'Miss Redburn'.
Chubby arms flailed in delight, and Ed ducked just in
time as Joe's plastic drinking cup rocketed across the
kitchen and clattered into the sink.

'Ed, what's going on?' Mrs Englefield shouted from the
hall. 'Are you practising your silly interviews on that
baby again?'

'Er, can't hear you, Mum. I'm off now, anyway. Be back
in time for dinner.' Giving his brother's snub nose a
grateful little tweak, Ed hissed goodbye, and slipped out,
his whole body tingling with excitement at the thought of
what he was about to attempt.

It was to be the scoop of a life-time!

As he pushed his bike down the front path, he tried to imagine what the real Miss Redburn would say when he finally confronted her . . .

'HEY, ED, YOU'RE UP EARLY! WE STILL GOING TO THAT JUDO EXHIBITION AT THE CIVIC CENTRE?'

The shrill voice of Cyril North, who lived next door to Ed, jerked him back to reality. Cyril had just finished his paper-round and, still perched on his bike, was leaning against one of the gate-posts. Clad in the old, bluey-green tracksuit that he usually wore at weekends, Cyril reminded Ed of a rather thin, wide-eyed budgie.

'Where are you off to at this hour of the morning, anyway?' Cyril went on curiously.

'I'm cycling over to Brays Copse,' Ed told him. 'There's a film unit on location at Cromwell's House, shooting some scenes for a new film.'

'Yeah, I heard about that,' said Cyril excitedly, skidding round and round on the pavement, and chattering away like a machine-gun. 'I was thinking of cycling over there myself . . . see if I could spot ole Fiona Blackburn.'

'You mean "Redburn",' said Ed, mounting his bike. Almost off-handedly he added, 'As a matter of fact, I'm going to interview her for the school magazine.'

There came a screech of brakes, as Cyril almost fell off his bike. Not for the first time in his life, he stared at Edward Englefield in open-mouthed awe. 'FIONA REDBURN?' he gasped.

'Yep.'

'But, she . . . she doesn't have anything to do with kids! She's a whopping great film star!'

'That's exactly why I'm going to interview her.' Anxious to be on his way, Ed was already cycling slowly

27

up the street. 'Well, are you coming or not, Northy?'

'No! I mean . . . don't be daft! They won't even let you in! I'll bet you don't get within a mile of her!'

'Bet I do.'

'You're *crazy*! You'll get arrested!' Cyril's voice began to fade as Ed gathered speed. 'Anyway, I haven't had my breakfast yet!'

Ed knew it was just an excuse. Whenever it came to something really daring Cyril suddenly remembered that it was time for some meal or other.

'I'LL COME IF YOU'LL WAIT TILL I'VE HAD MY BREKKERS!'

Cyril's distant, yelling figure vanished from sight, as Ed turned the corner, and set off through the estate. He'd tell his friend about it when he got back, anyway ... Watch Cyril's eyes bulge with awe, as Ed described how he had captured the incredible scoop which would have every kid in Baker Street School clamouring for a copy of the *Bugle*.

Ed's spirits soared as he sped through the outskirts of Chiverton, and out into the countryside. There had been a light fall of rain during the night, but now the world smelled fresh and vibrant in the first warmth of the climbing sun. Ed cycled a little faster. He was making a mental list of some questions to ask Miss Redburn, when there came a dull, metallic *Thunnng!* and his feet whizzed round with the speed of a racing-cyclist.

Ed groaned inwardly as he wobbled to a halt at the roadside. What with practising interviews on Baby Joe, and chatting with Cyril North, he had completely forgotten to check that weak link in his bicycle chain ... and now it had snapped.

He was still trying to mend it ten minutes later when a small red car drove up, and skidded to a halt alongside him. A cheerful, sprightly face, adorned with just a smear of black moustache, appeared at the near-side window.

' 'Allo, 'allo, young Ed!' said the face. 'Having a spot of bother, then?'

Ed knew Reg Holloway, the proprietor of Holloway's Minicabs, quite well because Reg often gave Mr Englefield a lift home from the station. If you wanted to be picked up somewhere in Chiverton, and dropped off somewhere else, Reg Holloway could usually manage it. But Ed was even more delighted to see him when he learned that Reg was also on his way to the film set.

29

It seemed that a boy of about Ed's age had a small part in the film, and Reg had been hired to drive the young actor out to Brays Copse each morning.

'Kid called Michael Allsop,' Reg went on, as he took a quick look at Ed's bike. 'Ever heard of him? No? Well, anyway, he was due to start filming this morning, but he's gone down with some kind of nervous rash. And his mother can't get in touch with the film unit, 'cos they're having bother with their telephone lines. Now don't you worry, I says to 'er. Old Reg'll nip over to Brays Copse, and tell the Director what's happened. So as you're going there, too, young Ed, you might as well hop in!'

Pausing only to conceal his bike in some bushes where it would be safe, Ed hopped in.

'Thanks for the lift, Mr Holloway,' he said gratefully, as they sped off with a clash of gears.

'Pleasure, my old son. Someone to talk to.' Reg winked and grinned at Ed's reflection in the rear-view mirror. 'Bet you're after her autograph, eh?'

'Whose autograph, Mr Holloway?'

'Why, Her Ladyship, of course. The Star of the film! The one-and-only Fiona!'

'Er, something like that,' Ed replied, trying to wipe off the chain-oil which had somehow oozed on to his arms.

'Well, you're welcome to it,' Reg was saying. 'She's been causing trouble on the set all week, so I hear. They reckon she's a right . . . pain in the neck!'

Reg launched into a description of Fiona Redburn's notorious tantrums, but Ed was too elated by this unexpected turn of events to pay much attention. Interviewing Fiona Redburn was one thing, but actually managing to smuggle himself on to a film set was quite another. There'd be police and security men just waiting to pounce on casual sight-seers, such as editors of school magazines. But now, thanks to that weak link in his bicycle-chain, the problem had been solved.

'Here we are!' chirped Reg, as they turned off the road, and in through some big, rickety iron gates, where a group of thickset men were chatting to a couple of policemen.

One of the policemen came over to speak to Reg, and Ed's heart missed a beat as the uniformed figure peered into the back of the car.

'Who's the boy?'

'Friend of mine,' Reg assured the officer. 'He's all right, mate, honest. I'll make sure he don't get into no mischief!'

To Ed's wild relief, they were driving on. And then the exciting bustle of a film unit on location began to unfold before his fascinated eyes.

There were cars and heavy vans parked all over the place. Men and women wearing jeans and duffle coats were tramping about in a sea of mud, most of them brandishing clip-boards, and steaming mugs of tea. Ed saw things that looked like miniature traffic-lights, and there seemed to be cameras everywhere – looming on metal stalks like one-eyed space-monsters. And dominating it all, was the ivy-covered façade of Cromwell's House.

Actually it was just a crumbling old mansion, which – according to rumour – had once been visited by Oliver Cromwell. Some people claimed that he had slept in it, others that he had hidden in it. Ed thought it more likely that Cromwell had bombarded it. But now, with the help of some cleverly arranged scenery, and a dash of paint, the old place looked quite impressive. Sort of . . . reborn.

'Wish they'd do a job like that on my bathroom,' Reg

remarked, as they stopped near a mobile canteen. 'Now you'd better sit tight, old son, while I go and find the Director and tell him what's happened. Shan't be long . . .!' Then he was gone, his ferrety figure darting away through the confusion of people and equipment.

But Ed had no intention of sitting tight. Somewhere out there was the walking, talking vision of loveliness that he had come to interview. He paused to check that pens, pencils, press cards and notepad were all in their proper places. Then he cautiously eased open the car door, and stepped out into an utter bedlam of noise.

He waited a moment for someone to bellow, 'HOY! WHAT'S THAT KID DOING 'ERE . . .?' But no one did. In fact no one paid any attention to him at all as he began to pick his way through the mud, stepping carefully over the heavy cables that seemed to criss-cross the whole area.

Until . . . quite suddenly . . . there she was, sweeping past in a cocoon of silvery-grey fur, her hair coiled like golden snakes above that haughty, unmistakable profile.

There was no hope of interviewing Miss Fiona Redburn at that moment, however, for she was surrounded by a little crowd of shouting, gesticulating people, who seemed to be begging and pleading with the great actress.

'Please, Fiona! I know it's difficult without the boy, but we almost got it that time! Just one more take!'

'No!' The golden snakes tossed angrily. 'And as for that oaf of a director, he couldn't direct traffic up a one-way street! It's no wonder I'm a bag of nerves!'

'But, Fiona . . .'

'LEAVE ME ALONE!' screamed the star of *Love on a Luncheon Voucher*. Ed saw her flounce up the steps of a long, white-painted caravan. As the door slammed shut behind her, a baffled groan went up, and one or two people threw down their clip-boards in disgust.

It was obvious to Ed that it was going to take a lot more begging and pleading to persuade Miss Redburn to come out again. By then, someone might have noticed him and handed him over to one of those scruffy giants at the main gates. So there was only one solution – he had to corner this wild, proud creature in her own den.

When he was certain that no one was watching him, Ed began to slide around one end of the caravan. To his relief, there was no one on the other side. Just a strip of mud, and some bushes in which a few empty wooden crates had been dumped.

Ed eyed the crates thoughtfully. Now if he stood one of them against the side of the caravan, he might just be able to reach that window at the far end . . .

At that precise moment, the 'wild, proud creature' was stalking up and down, listening with smug satisfaction to the angry hubbub outside the door of the caravan. Let them wait, she thought savagely. She'd make that idiot of a director go down on his bended knees before she so much as faced another camera. It wasn't her fault that the film was behind schedule. That ghastly house gave her the creeps, and now that grotty kid Allsop hadn't turned up.

Miss Redburn was aiming a petulant kick at the nearest piece of furniture, when she heard a strange scraping sound . . . followed by a faint creak.

Something bumped against the rear wall of the caravan, just outside the window. And then, to her stupefied amazement, an oil-streaked face rose up into view, and pressed itself against the dusty pane.

A small card appeared alongside the face, and then a muffled voice called, ''scuse me, Miss Redburn. My name's Englefield, and I'm here on behalf of the *Baker Street Bugle* . . .'

'*AAAAAAAHIEEEEE!*'

Startled by the sheer power and intensity of that horrified scream, Ed lost his balance, slipped, and fell backwards off the crate into a deep patch of cloying mud. He slithered to his feet, leaving a little trail of pens and

press cards, and scuttled back round the end of the caravan . . . only to see that Miss Redburn had beaten him to
it. She must have wrenched open the door with frenzied
speed, and hurled herself into the throng of film people.

Ed could hear her screaming something about a Peeping Tom. 'He was pulling faces at me, I tell you! Oh, it
was HORRIBLE! I nearly died on the spot! I want him
found, do you hear? Tracked down and locked up like the
beast that he is!'

Ed was beginning to feel a little irritated by Miss

Redburn's tantrums. He was about to make a tactical retreat to consider his next move, when a heavy hand fell on his shoulder, and a voice rasped, 'Now what little hole in the ground did YOU pop up from? Grubby little urchins aren't allowed on film sets, you know!'

Ed's captor was a tall bony man, with a twitching, bearded face. He was glaring down at the editor of the *Bugle* through a pair of sinister, rimless dark glasses. 'Where did you COME from, I said?'

Racking his brains for an answer, Ed looked round wildly, and pointed at Reg Holloway's car, which was still parked near the mobile canteen.

'You've just arrived in that car? The one marked "Holloway's Minicabs"?'

As Ed nodded brightly, Dark Glasses turned, and let out a yell of relief. 'IT'S THE BOY – YOUNG ALLSOP! HE'S TURNED UP AT LAST!'

There was a rush of feet, and everything seemed to go dark as a ring of bodies surrounded Ed. Heads craned to peer at the small, bedraggled figure.

'Are you sure it's young Allsop?' someone asked. 'I mean, the only person who knows what he looks like is the Casting Director ...'

'... and he cleared off yesterday after that row with Fiona', someone else sighed.

'Anyway, how can you tell *what* he looks like under all that mud and oil?' Dark Glasses snapped impatiently.

'Yeah! Look at it! Just right for the part – he must have come straight from the make-up department!'

'So what are we waiting for?' shouted Dark Glasses. Several hands grabbed Ed and began to haul him along. 'Let's get this scene in the can before Fiona locks herself in the caravan again!'

Everything happened very quickly after that. Make-up girls fussed around Ed, sticking bits of straw in his hair, and daubing even more black stuff on his face. He deduced from the renewed bedlam of shouts and yells that Fiona Redburn had been persuaded to go through with the next scene, on condition that Dark Glasses directed her. Apparently the real director had developed a splitting headache, combined with double-vision, and retired to his hotel in Chiverton.

Then, without quite knowing how, Ed found himself standing in front of Cromwell's House, trapped in a metal forest of spotlights and cameras, with Dark Glasses looming over him.

'Right, young Allsop. I'll give you a brief run-down on this scene, just to remind you what it's all about . . .'

Ed couldn't see much point in explaining that he wasn't Michael Allsop. Not just yet, anyway. The film people seemed to have enough trouble on their plate. And apart from that, he sensed that this might be his last chance to interview Fiona Redburn.

'Your father ran off with a shorthand-typist,' Dark Glasses was saying, 'and you haven't seen your mother since she abandoned you as a baby on the steps of a Chinese Take-Away, owned by a Mr and Mrs Wong. They take pity on you, and bring you up as their own child . . . until the day you run away, determined to track down your real mother . . .' Dark Glasses paused for breath '. . . who was last heard of working for an aristocratic family as a cleaning woman, in that house.'

Dark Glasses pointed at the massive front doors of Cromwell's House, and droned on, 'You've tramped for hundreds of miles to get here. A waif of the world. Buffeted by storms, and spurned by long-distance lorry drivers. But now, as the scene opens, your nightmarish ordeal is nearing its end ...'

Ed had listened intently. He was beginning to realise why the film was called *The Return of Nigel Wong*.

'Okay, son?' Dark Glasses had turned away, and was scurrying back to the array of cameras. 'Just sob and whimper a bit, and let Miss Redburn do the acting. ALL RIGHT, EVERYBODY ... POSITIONS PLEASE! THIS IS A TAKE!'

A youth charged up, and almost snapped off Ed's nose with a clack of his clapper-board. 'Scene twenty-seven, take four!' he shouted.

'Mark it!' yelled a cameraman.

'ACTION!' boomed Dark Glasses.

Cameras whirred, and then the doors of Cromwell's House flew open. There stood Fiona, her magnificent figure swathed in a tawdry dress. Her face was pale and anxious, but, thanks to the skill of the make-up department, still a face of breath-taking beauty.

'Don't say anything! Just don't say ANYTHING!' she gasped, her voice distraught with pretended agony.

Ed didn't say anything as Fiona started to advance down the steps, her eyes fixed on the editor of the *Bugle*, the cameras devouring her every movement. 'I know it's you – that ... that little scrap of life that I abandoned so many years ago! I can tell by the way you're just ... *standing* there, with that accusing look in your eyes!'

It all sounded a bit daft to Ed, but he hadn't come all this way just to pass judgment on Miss Redburn's acting ability. He was reaching inside his shirt for his notepad, when Fiona suddenly flew down the steps, and scooped him into her arms, smothering him in musky odours,

and, to Ed's mild surprise, a definite whiff of extra-strong mints.

'My poor, poor darling,' Fiona sobbed, burying her face in his chest. '*Say* something ... ANYTHING! Tell me what's in your heart!'

'Well, I tried to speak to you just now, Miss Redburn,' Ed began, struggling in the vice-like grip to pull out one of his press cards. 'Sorry if I gave you a fright, looking through your window like that – but I'm not really

Michael Allsop, y'see ... I'm the editor of our school magazine, and ...'

'School magazine?' Ed's voice was drowned by a chorus of puzzled cries. 'What's he on about?'

'This isn't in the script!'

'And what's he doing with that notebook? There's nothing in this scene about a notebook!'

'CUT!' roared Dark Glasses frantically. 'GET THAT KID AWAY FROM FIONA!'

But it was too late. Miss Redburn had lifted her face and was staring at Ed in horrified recognition.

'It's *him*!' she screamed. 'The face at the window! IT'S THE PEEPING TOM!'

Ed flopped down into the mud again as the actress snatched her arms away, and leapt back as if she had been stung.

'You BEASTS!' she howled hysterically, her cries directed at the film crew in general. 'You KNEW he wasn't the Allsop kid! You knew it all the time! It was just a TRICK to humiliate me!'

'You're out of your tiny mind!' bawled Dark Glasses rushing forward, and almost tripping over Ed who was crawling for the shelter of a nearby tea-trolley. 'Now if you'll just calm down for a minute ...'

'Don't you tell me what to do, you ... you FOUR-EYED CREEP!' Miss Redburn's flailing hands slammed against Dark Glasses' chest, sending him staggering back into a little queue of spotlights. Glass shattered, and sparks crackled, as the spotlights toppled like a row of ninepins. Technicians scattered and collided, and someone yelled for the generator to be switched off.

And through it all, tottered a golden-haired figure, with a strange, trance-like expression on its face. It was

Fiona – heading, once again, for the sanctuary of her cara-van.

'That does it!' roared Dark Glasses. 'That just about corks the bottle! I wouldn't work with that ... that ... CRUMMY ... BAD TEMPERED ... PAIN IN THE NECK if they offered me a percentage of the profits!'

Dark Glasses' words suddenly reminded Ed of Reg Holloway. In all, it seemed an appropriate moment to work his way back to the car. None of the film people tried to stop him. They were far too busy dismantling equipment, and winding up cables. Ed was surprised to see that some of them were actually smiling, as if some great weight had been lifted from their shoulders.

'She's gone too far this time,' he heard one of them say. 'I wouldn't be surprised if they hired a new female lead.'

'Let's hope so,' said another. 'Another week like this and we would have gone stark, raving bonkers – the whole lot of us! You know what? I reckon that kid did us a favour!'

Ed had mixed feelings about that last remark, as he climbed into Reg Holloway's minicab. He was gazing ruefully at his empty notepad, when Reg himself ap-peared, squeezing in behind the steering-wheel. He apologised profusely to Ed for taking so long.

'Couldn't find the bloomin' Director,' Reg explained, as they drove off. 'So I had a quick cuppa in the mobile canteen. Then one of the technicians came in, and said they were all going home!' Reg chuckled knowingly. 'I wouldn't mind betting it's got something to do with Her Ladyhip,' he said, easing the car through the chaos of a film unit that was packing its bags. 'I told yer she was a bad 'un!'

As they drove out through the main gates, Ed caught a

last glimpse of Dark Glasses, hammering on the door of Fiona Redburn's caravan.

'Anyway,' Reg Holloway prattled on, 'I left a message about young Allsop being taken poorly, and told 'em to get in touch with his mother. I mean, I can't do much more than that, can I?'

'I guess not, Mr Holloway,' said Ed. He was consoling himself with the thought that he still had the best part of a month in which to save the *Bugle* from extinction. Perhaps he would write an article about his brief, but sensational career as a film actor. And then again, perhaps he wouldn't. Ed doubted if even Cyril North would believe it . . .

'STROLL ON, YOUNG ED! 'Reg Holloway's voice exploded through the car. He was goggling at Ed's reflection in the rear-view mirror, as if noticing for the first time that his passenger was caked with make-up and mud from head to foot.

'I reckon they ought to make a film about you! I've never known any kid get in a state like that, just from sitting in the back of a car!'

A present from Mrs Noah

It wasn't often that Baby Joe Englefield had a grizzle, but when he did, it was a grizzle to be remembered. As Karen had once put it, 'He really goes to town.' And as if in sympathy with the plight of the *Bugle*, Baby Joe went to town the following Monday morning, summing up his opinion of the world, and everybody in it, with a mighty, ear-splitting *'WHUUUAAAAAAAHH!'*

The nerve-rending sound followed Ed and Cyril down the street, as they cycled off to school. 'I don't think I've heard any baby yell as loudly as your Joe,' said Cyril in amazement. 'What's he yelling about this time?'

'Nobody knows,' said Ed. 'He's just sort of gets fed up, and starts yelling. It goes on for days sometimes. He just yells, an' yells, an'—'

'Hey, *that's* an idea,' Cyril cut in excitedly. 'You could do a sort of survey on it for the school mag!'

'A survey on what?'

'*Baby-yelling!* I mean, suppose you made a list of the different kinds of yells, and found out what starts 'em. I bet thousands of mothers would buy the *Bugle*, just to find out what makes their babies yell, so's they'd know how to stop 'em.' Cyril paused for breath. 'Just think of it,

44

Ed ... you might become an expert on baby-yelling!'

'One of these days, Northy, you'll become an expert on thinking up daft ideas.'

'Well, *I* think it's a good idea,' Cyril persisted. 'There's no harm trying it, is there? I mean, you're going to need something really sensational, now that your interview with Fiona Redburn was a flop.'

'It wasn't a flop,' retorted Ed. 'I keep telling you that I ...'

Ed's voice trailed away. It was just no use trying to convince his friend that he had actually stood on a film-set, and been hugged by Fiona Redburn. And in a way, Cyril was right. The whole affair *had* been a flop, for all he had got out of it was a telling-off from his parents for coming home like a miniature tramp, pushing a bike with a broken chain. At that precise moment, the *Bugle* seemed utterly doomed.

Ed's spirits were sinking lower and lower, when Cyril suddenly thumped him on the shoulder, and yelled, *'Ed, look at that! Valerie Pigden's having another demonstration!'*

The gates of Baker Street School had come into view, and marching up and down in front of them was a lean, pony-tailed figure, holding aloft a hockey-stick, to which was nailed a large, home-made banner.

'HANDS OFF MRS NOAH!' declared the banner, in black, spidery letters. And 'SUPPORT MY CAMPAIGN TO OPPOSE THIS BUREAUCRATIC TYRANNY!'

Valerie Pigden always seemed to be demonstrating about something. Ed's father had described her as a 'Junior Urban Guerilla' – or, as Ed had explained to Cyril, someone who liked stirring things up.

'What's the demo-demon on about now?' Ed asked, as

he joined Johnny Rackham and some of his pals, who were watching the demonstration from the relative safety of the playground.

'Cats and dogs,' chuckled Johnny. 'She's trying to get up a petition to stop the council from chucking that old woman out of her house. You know, the one with all the animals.'

'They reckon she'd take in an elephant if someone tied it to her gate post,' another boy chimed in. 'It's no wonder they call her "Mrs Noah"!'

Of course! thought Ed, with a stir of excitement. Mrs Noah! The old lady who had opened her doors to the refugees of the animal world. Waifs and strays, and unwanted family pets. Take them along to Mrs Noah, and she would gladly provide them with a home.

But as her army of creatures had grown, so had the bedlam of barks, and squawks, and grunts which tormented her neighbours by night and day. So, in the face of bitter complaints, the Chiverton Borough Council had delivered a grim ultimatum. Unless Mrs Noah disposed of her animals forthwith, she would have to be evicted.

'. . . Why should Mrs Noah have to suffer, just because she's kind, and she loves animals?' Valerie Pigden was shouting. 'Those heartless monsters at the Town Hall haven't offered to adopt any of her little friends, have they? Or find good homes for them!'

'I wonder if Mrs Noah's got any parrots?' said Cyril in a hushed voice, in case Valerie heard him. 'I wouldn't mind adopting a parrot!'

'*And if Mrs Noah refuses to move out,*' Valerie thundered on, '*all those poor unfortunate creatures will probably be put to sleep. And it's not just the lives of cats and*

*dogs that are at stake.There's white mice, budgies, guinea-
pigs and jerbils . . .!'*

Someone giggled at the back of the crowd of watching
children. 'Sounds like a firm of solicitors!'

'Sounds more to me like a line from a well-known
popular song,' whooped Johnny Rackham, grabbing
Cyril by the shoulders and waltzing him around.
'Guinea-pigs and jerbils, and big balls of string,' he sang
tunelessly, until there came a sudden yell of 'LOOK
OUT! HERE SHE COMES!'

Valerie's audience scattered like wind-blown leaves as
she came marching across the playground. But her target
was Ed. She managed to corner the Editor of the *Bugle*
half-way to the bike-sheds, demanding that he sign her
petition.

'Sorry, Valerie. As Editor of the *Bugle*, I can't appear
to be taking sides. All I can do is report the facts.'

'You mean you're frightened to face up to the realities
of urban tyranny, Ed Englefield,' Valerie snapped. 'All
right, then. I'll write an article for the *Bugle*, attacking
the Council for its persecution of Mrs Noah. Or maybe
you'd like to see her hounded out of her home by those
faceless brutes at the Town Hall?'

'It's . . . er, not a question of that,' Ed said evasively.
Valerie's last contribution to the *Bugle* was still a painful
memory, for it had contained an attack on Mrs Goodenough, who was notorious for confiscating sweets and
comics in class. Valerie had accused her of secretly eating
the sweets, and selling the comics to other children at half
price. To Ed's dismay, Mrs Goodenough had taken the
article seriously, and he had only saved the *Bugle* by publishing an abject apology to the angry tutor, and offering
to clean her Yamaha. So his caution was understandable.

'Tell you what, Valerie,' he went on, 'if you'll let me have a synopsis of the article, I promise I'll—'

'I don't want promises!' Valerie snapped. 'I want a decision NOW! Where's your moral courage, Englefield?'

To Ed's relief, the roll-call whistle saved his moral courage from being put to the test, and he was able to escape from Valerie in the general rush.

But the 'Demo-demon' had given him an idea – a story for the *Bugle* that would provoke more Human Interest than a hundred Fiona Redburns!

He told Cyril about it during morning break.

'You're going to interview Mrs Noah, and get all her pets adopted?' gasped Cyril.

'Why not?' said Ed, scribbling on his notepad, listing questions he was going to put to Mrs Noah. 'It might

work. Y'see, instead of attacking the Council, I'm going
to write about the plight of Mrs Noah's pets. It'll be a sort
of campaign by the *Bugle* to get the pets adopted. I might
even adopt one of 'em myself, if I can talk my parents
into it.'

'And I'll adopt a parrot!' Cyril cried excitedly. 'There's
just one problem,' he added ominously.

'What's that?'

'Valerie Pigden! Soon as she sees the article, she'll say
it was her idea in the first place. She'll go potty! She . . .
she'll probably get up a demonstration against YOU, Ed!'

'No she won't,' said Ed, 'because she'll have no reason
to.' He had already decided that if Valerie forgot about
attacking the Council, and concentrated on saving Mrs
Noah's pets, he would allow her to collaborate on the
article.

'We'll wait for her after school and tell her what I'm
going to do. Then she won't have any complaints, will
she?'

But Ed didn't get a chance to inform Valerie of his
plans. As he and Cyril were collecting their bikes after
school, they saw her wiry, restless figure vanishing
through the main gates, as if in some tremendous hurry.

'Makes no difference,' Ed said confidently, as they
cycled off. 'If I show her an outline of the article before
it's published, she can't accuse me of going behind her
back. So let's go see Mrs Noah . . .'

In preparation for the day that he would become a top-
flight reporter, Ed had already charted the whereabouts of
every street and avenue in Chiverton, so he knew exactly
where Mrs Noah lived. He had packed a fresh notebook,
printed some new press cards, and brought along his

camera to take some photographs of the old lady, posing poignantly amidst her array of animals.

In fact, as they turned into Mrs Noah's street, there seemed to be animals everywhere!

Animals *and* people! People in ones, and twos, and even whole famiies. All wandering along in a happy bedlam of laughter, barks, mews, and chirrups. They saw cats in baskets, and budgies in cages. Puppies squirmed in the arms of flushed, delighted children.

'Where the heck are they all coming from?' gasped Cyril, as a car drove past with what looked like a pig sitting in the back seat.

Ed had a good idea, but he was trying hard not to think about it. Just ahead of them, a boy came out of a gate, carrying a bowl which contained a large goldfish. 'Thanks a lot, Mrs Noah,' he called. 'I won't forget to feed him, and I promise I'll bring him to visit you every week.' With a final wave he hurried off, just as Ed and Cyril cycled up, and saw Mrs Noah standing at the gate. She had an enormous ginger cat draped over one shoulder, and her small, bright-eyed face peeped out at them from beneath a faded yellow head-scarf.

'You're just in time, boys,' she beamed. 'I've got *one* little dearie left!'

Ed and Cyril stared at each other wordlessly, then at the rambling, overgrown garden that surrounded Mrs Noah's cottage. Here and there among the trees they saw kennels, and bird-houses, and little wire compounds, all empty and silent now ... their former occupants, at that very moment, departing to all parts of Chiverton.

'I'm afraid you can't have the Duchess,' Mrs Noah was saying, fondling and kissing the ginger cat. 'She's my very own, special pet. Aren't you, Duchess?' She suddenly

opened the gate and beckoned to Ed. 'Well, come on in, my dear. Don't be shy!'

Leaving Cyril peeping nervously over the ramshackle front fence, Ed wandered in. Although the *Bugle*'s 'Save-The-Animals' campaign was clearly in ruins, perhaps there was another story behind the reason for all those empty compounds. It was his only hope now.

'Ask her if the one she's got left is a parrot,' came a hiss from behind him. Ed ignored Cyril, and took out his notebook.

'Actually, ma'am,' he began, 'I haven't come to adopt a dearie . . . I mean, a pet. I'm from the *Baker Street Bugle*, y'see, and—'

'Not *another* newspaper?' cried Mrs Noah. She peered curiously at Ed's small, mop-haired figure. 'You reporters seem to be getting younger and younger these days. But perhaps you're one of those "cub" reporters, out on his first little adventure, eh? Anyway, I'm afraid you're too late . . . the *Chronicle* has already done me!'

'The *Chronicle*, ma'am? You mean the *Chiverton Chronicle*?'

'That's right, dear. Two of their gentlemen came round yesterday evening.' Mrs Noah put down the ginger cat, and dragged a crumpled newspaper from the pocket of her cardigan.

Sure enough, it was a copy of the afternoon edition of the *Chronicle*. And there, on the feature page, was an article about Mrs Noah, highlighting the terrible threat that hung over her little army of waifs and strays.

Ed was beginning to realise what had happened. The afternoon edition of the *Chronicle* had, as usual, gone on sale at lunch-time. All that day, even as Ed was planning his wonderful campaign, the animal-lovers of Chiverton must have been reading the article, and rushing to the aid of Mrs Noah and her pets. No wonder there was only one little dearie left.

'I shall miss them all dreadfully,' sighed Mrs Noah. 'Especially Henry. Oh, you should have seen him, young man ... dangling by his tail from the lampshade ... pelting the Duchess with pieces of bacon rind.'

'Henry, ma'am?'

'The little monkey that I took in from the bankrupt zoo,' Mrs Noah explained. 'I was absolutely dreading the thought of having to hand him over to one of those animal rescue places, although I know they do their best. But he'll be safe and happy in his new home now. They *all* will. And it's all thanks to that wonderful little girl!'

'Er ... what little girl, ma'am?' Ed asked, his heart missing a beat or two.

'*This* little girl!' snapped a familiar voice. Ed glanced past Mrs Noah at the lean, pony-tailed figure which had appeared in the doorway of the house.

'IT'S VALERIE PIGDEN!' yelled Cyril from the street. 'That's why she was in such a big hurry after school, Ed! She was heading for Mrs Noah's!'

'Oh, you know each other, then?' beamed Mrs Noah. 'Then perhaps I've no need to tell you that it was Valerie who telephoned the Editor of the *Chronicle* yesterday morning, and protested about the Council's threat to evict me unless I disposed of my little friends!'

'And *that's* why they sent the reporters round,' Valerie cut in acidly. 'The *Chronicle* sensed that there was a good story in poor Mrs Noah! Just like you, Ed Englefield! Why, you sneaky little thing! I *thought* you might try something like this!'

'I'm not sneaky,' protested Ed. 'I was going to discuss

the article with you before I went to press. You ask Cyril.'

'No thanks. I expect he's just as sneaky as you are. Anyway, if you're *really* worried about Mrs Noah's pets, there's still a chance to do something about it. As she just told you, there's one left!'

'Don't be daft,' said Ed, backing hastily towards the gate. 'I can't go around adopting animals without asking my parents.'

'And I was only joking about adopting a parrot,' Cyril called frantically.

But it was too late. Cupping her hands to her mouth, Valerie let out a shrill cry that sounded something like '*CHARLEEEEEEEE!*'

From somewhere behind the house, came a deep, answering 'WAWWRRF!' They heard a sound like a baby rhino, crashing and panting through undergrowth . . . growing louder, and louder. And then a large, reddish-brown shape skidded around the corner of the house, and threw itself at Ed.

As he went down under a smother of paws, and snorting nostrils, it felt as if all the dogs in the world were trampling all over him, and trying to lick his face off. Fighting for breath, Ed thought he heard Cyril say, 'I'd, er . . . better be off home now, Ed. I'll get into trouble if I miss my tea . . .'

Then Mrs Noah cried out, 'No, Charles! NO! Come to heel, you naughty boy!'

The crushing weight lifted from Ed's body. For a moment he lay there, wondering if any bones had been broken. His camera seemed to be intact, although it was now wrapped around his neck, and his notebook seemed to be suspended in mid-air, a few feet away. As Ed's eyes

cleared, he saw that it was gripped in the floppy jaws of the biggest boxer dog he had ever seen.

'Are you all right, young man?' Mrs Noah asked anxiously, taking a firmer grip on the dog's collar. 'It's just his little way of giving everyone a warm welcome, you see. He's ever so friendly, really!'

'And he's very good with children,' said Valerie.

He's good at knocking them down, Ed thought, eyeing the massive dog warily. In the absence of a proper tail, its whole body was wagging eagerly, and it was clearly poised to 'welcome' him again, should Mrs Noah loosen her grip.

'He's got ever such a good pedigree,' she went on. 'His real name is Charlesworthy Sunnysides Badminton the Fourth. But I call him Charles, for short. And if you want him,' she added hopefully, 'he's all yours!'

'No thanks, Mrs Noah!' Ed said hastily, retreating towards the gate again. 'I mean, I'd like to take him, but our garden isn't big enough. A dog like that would need a field to play in. And . . . and anyway, I'd never get him home on my bike!'

'*That's just an excuse, Ed Englefield!*' Valerie's voice rang out. '*I* can bring your bike home!'

'I . . . I know you can, but—'

'If someone doesn't adopt Charles, he'll have to be sent to one of those homes . . . or be put to sleep, because Mrs Noah can't afford to keep him any longer. Is *that* what you want? IS IT?' Valerie's voice swelled to a peak of accusing fury. 'If you turn your back on Mrs Noah now . . . I'LL TELL EVERYONE AT SCHOOL THAT YOU WERE GOING TO EXPLOIT THIS POOR OLD LADY, JUST TO GET A STORY FOR THE *BUGLE*!'

'That's not true,' said Ed indignantly. 'I was going to bring her plight to everyone's attention . . . just like the *Chronicle* did. Anyway,' he went on desperately, 'there's plenty of time. Someone might still come along, and—'

Ed broke off as a kind of pleading little whine came from Charlesworthy Sunnysides Badminton the Fourth. He was sitting quietly now, his big brown eyes fixed on Ed. On his black-and-white face there was an expression which clearly said, 'I'm well looked after here, but I'd love to be owned by a boy who would take me for walks, and have a wrestle now and then. I can play football with my nose, too. Honest, I can!'

Ed groaned inwardly, and closed his eyes. For one, terrible moment, he had a vision of his parents being 'welcomed' by Charles. Then he opened his eyes, and said helplessly, 'You'll have to follow me on my bike then, Valerie.'

'HE'S GOING TO ADOPT HIM!' Valerie screamed.

Charging back into the house, she re-emerged with a massive chain lead. Somehow, Charles was held down while Mrs Noah bade him a tearful farewell, and the lead was clipped to his collar.

'You'll remember this day as long as you live, Ed Englefield,' yelled Valerie, shoving the other end of the lead into Ed's sweaty hand. 'The day you made an old lady very happy, and gained a lifelong friend!'

The 'lifelong friend' seemed to know that he had just been adopted, for he dropped Ed's notebook, threw a last, grateful glance at Mrs Noah, then shot out of the gate. Ed had no choice but to follow, at some speed, for the sudden jerk had tightened the strap of the lead around his wrist.

'Don't forget to give him his vitamin chockie drops,' cried Mrs Noah, waving and smiling tearfully, as Ed vanished up the street. Then she was gone, and Ed was concentrating on the task of trying to keep at least one foot on the pavement, as Charlesworthy Sunnysides Badminton the Fourth went bounding joyfully through the streets of Chiverton.

Ed had a blurred impression of people scattering from his path. He whizzed past shops, houses, sidestreets, a recreation ground, and something that looked like Cyril North, before Charles ran out of steam, and skidded to a merciful halt. Long pink tongue lolling out, he was staring questioningly at Ed as if to say, 'Where to now, master?' when a goggle-eyed Cyril came cycling up.

'Hi, Ed,' Cyril said, halting at a safe distance from the

panting Charles, 'I, er . . . thought I'd better hang around, and find out what happened.'

'That was *very* brave of you, Northy,' breathed Ed, leaning exhaustedly against a wall. 'And it's just as well you did, 'cos now you can help me to get him home.'

'Home?' echoed Cyril.

As if responding to a command, Charles took off again. And so did Ed.

'What do you want to take it home for?' shouted Cyril, pedalling hard to keep up.

'Because it's mine!'

'IT'S *WHAT?*'

'Never mind! I'll explain as we go along . . .'

Afterwards, Ed could never quite remember how they had accomplished it. Somehow, with the help of Cyril's bike, and Charles' diminishing energy, they managed to steer the huge dog in the general direction of the Englefields' home, until, at long last, two exhausted, bedraggled boys, and a weary, but happy boxer arrived outside the front gate of Number 19 Avon Close.

'Now what do we do?' gasped Cyril, as soon as he had got his breath back. 'I mean, you can't just walk in there with a whopping great dog, Ed. Your mum and dad will go barmy!'

'Not if I can break it to them gently,' croaked Ed, anxiously scanning the house. To his relief, the back garden seemed to be deserted. He might just be able to reach the garden shed unseen, and hide Charles inside it. Then he could wait until the family was settled around the television, before casually bringing up the subject of Mrs Noah's four-legged gift. That way, his parents might be persuaded to allow Charles to stop the night, before finding a new home for him.

'I'd keep you if it was up to me, fella,' Ed told Charles, ruffling the boxer's ears. It was as if the running battle through the streets of Chiverton had formed a kind of bond between them. 'Honest, I would. But you know what parents are! Anyway, I'll put in a good word for you.'

Charles licked Ed's hand as if he understood. And he seemed to realise what was at stake, for he kept as quiet as a mouse as Ed led him through the front gate, and crept towards the house, leaving Cyril crouching nervously in the shelter of a shrub. 'Good luck, Ed,' he hissed.

'I'm going to need it,' thought Ed. As he passed the back door he heard a shrill, unwavering wail, coming from somewhere inside. It was Baby Joe ... still yelling, although a trifle hoarsely now. Perhaps that explained the absence of Englefields. They were all in the house, trying to soothe Baby Joe.

'Keep it up, baby brother!' Ed muttered to himself, as he crept up to the garden shed. Very quietly he slipped Charles' lead, and eased open the door. But before he

59

could say, 'In you go, boy,' the dog pricked up its ears, and bounded into the shed with its mighty, welcoming 'WAWWRRF!'

It was followed by a startled 'YAAOWWGH!' And then out of the shed shot Mr Englefield, in a fluttering explosion of files and papers, hotly pursued by Charles.

Ed watched in horrified silence as they completed two circuits of the garden, which ended with his father diving into the greenhouse, and slamming the door behind him.

'Here, Charles ... here, boy,' shouted Ed. But Charles was already making for the house. Like any dog with a raging thirst, he knew, from experience, that water was to be found in houses. Before Ed could reach him, he had skidded across the patio, and vanished through the French windows.

An instant later, following another pandemonium of crashes and screams, Mrs Englefield and Karen came tumbling through the back door.

'George *do* something!' screamed Mrs Englefield. 'There's a horrible great bloodhound rampaging through the house!'

'It's not a bloodhound, Mum,' said Ed, 'it's a boxer. And it's only trying to be friendly.'

'Friendly?' stormed Mr Englefield, clambering from the greenhouse. 'It almost killed me! What's the world coming to when a man can't get in a peaceful hour's office work in his own shed?'

'I didn't know you were in there, Dad.'

'I was trying to escape from your brother's yelling! And what happens? I get attacked by a mad dog! Look at my files ... *my schedules*!'

'*BABY JOE!*' screamed Mrs Englefield.

They all looked at her.

'He's still in the house – at the mercy of that MON-STER!'

'Maybe it's already got him,' gasped Karen. 'Listen!'

They all listened.

'He's stopped yelling,' said Ed.

'Oh, good grief!' groaned Mr Englefield.

Grabbing a wooden mallet from the shed, he led the rush into the house. But Baby Joe Englefield wasn't in any danger. Not from Charlesworthy Sunnysides Badminton the Fourth, anyway.

The big dog was sitting rigidly beside Joe's high-chair, eyes glued to the piece of chocolate biscuit that the fascinated baby was thrusting down at him. Very deliberately, but very gently for such a large dog, he eased the gooey fragment from Joe's chubby fingers . . . chomped, gulped, and smacked his lips, as if devouring a leg of lamb . . . before resuming his rigid, expectant posture.

Apart from the lip-smackings, and Joe's chuckles, the whole operation had taken place in utter silence.

'It's magic,' breathed Karen.

'Incredible,' whispered Mrs Englefield.

'I told you he was friendly,' said Ed.

'HE'S DROOLING ALL OVER THE CARPET!' shouted Mr Englefield. Brandishing the mallet in one hand, he grabbed Charles' lead, and began to drag him towards the French windows. 'Messy great brute! I don't care *how* much the baby likes him, he's going back where he came from!'

'*WHUUUAAAAAHHHHHH*!'

Mr Englefield dropped the lead as if he had been stung, as Baby Joe let rip again. This time the nerve-rending din slowly died to a delighted gurgle, as Charles crept back to the high-chair, and froze into a patient, begging statue.

A massive sigh of relief went up from the Englefields.

'Well, that settles it,' said Mrs Englefield, in a hushed voice. 'The dog will have to stay – even if only for a couple of days – until Baby Joe has settled down again.'

'Now just a minute, Rosemary—' Mr Englefield began.

'It's the only way, Dad,' said Karen. 'Think of all that lovely peace and quiet! I'll be able to catch up with my homework.'

'And you won't have to check your schedules in the shed,' said Ed.

'But he . . . he'll cost a *fortune* to feed!'

'We can cancel one of the papers,' said Mrs Englefield. In her most cajoling voice she added, 'It's only for a couple of days, George.'

Mr Englefield just stood there, his mouth opening and closing like a defeated, despairing goldfish.

'All right,' he spluttered at last. 'ALL RIGHT! But I'm not paying for his licence. Ed will have to pay for it out of his pocket-money. And the brute will have to sleep in the garage. I am not, repeat, NOT having him drooling over the fitted carpet!'

As Mr Englefield stormed out into the garden, Ed looked at his mother. 'It sounds as if Charles is staying for good, Mum. I mean, there's no point buying a licence for him if he isn't going to live with us, is there?'

'I shouldn't think so, darling.' Mrs Englfield was beaming at Baby Joe, who had just dropped another tiny piece of biscuit into Charles' cavernous, waiting jaws. 'As soon as your father gets over the shock, we'll find a nice, big basket, and move him into the kitchen.'

'Who . . . *Dad*?' cried Karen.

'You know very well what I mean, cheeky. Er . . . what did you say his name was, Ed?'

'Charlesworthy Sunnysides Badminton the Fourth. But Mrs Noah calls him Charles, for short.'

'Who's Mrs Noah, dear?'

'It's a long story, Mum,' said Ed, making for the door. 'Tell you all about it after tea. I'd better go and see if Valerie Pigden has brought my bike back . . .'

Valerie had, in fact, been and gone, leaving Ed's bike in the charge of Cyril, who was still hanging around ouside.

'Well, your trip to Mrs Noah's place wasn't a *complete* waste of time,' said Cyril, after Ed had explained how Charlesworthy Sunnysides Badminton the Fourth had found a new home. 'You've lost a story for the *Bugle*, but gained a big boxer!'

Ed nodded ruefully. In all the excitement he had almost forgotten that he was no closer to unearthing the Searing Human Drama that might save the *Bugle*.

'You might have gained a girl-friend, too, Ed,' Cyril went on slyly.

'Girl-friend?'

'Valerie Pigden! I reckon she fancies you, Ed. You've

become a sort of hero to her, adopting Charles the Fourth like that. She said to tell you that she doesn't really think you're sneaky, and that she's willing to organise a demonstration in support of the *Bugle*.'

That'll be the day, thought Ed, with an inward shudder. The prospect of being singled out as the object of Valerie Pigden's affections seemed almost as disastrous as losing the *Bugle* . . .

The Cruncher comes to town

As Mrs Englefield had predicted it wasn't long before
Charles the Fourth was equipped with a licence, and oc-
cupying a gigantic basket in a corner of the kitchen. The
family grew quite accustomed to tripping over him. Even
Mr Englefield was prepared to put up with a little incon-
venience, as long as Baby Joe's grizzles were kept to a mini-
mum. And apart from that, a fresh crisis had loomed.

As the weeks passed, and Ed failed to unearth the sensational story that would boost the circulation of the
Bugle, he became more and more depressed. Not even a
game of table tennis in the garage with his father could
relieve Ed's frustration. After being struck twice over the
left eyebrow with wild, backhand smashes, Mr Englefield
threw down his bat, and rapped, 'Right, my lad, this nonsense has gone far enough! It's time we held a council of
war!'

The 'council of war' took place that same evening,
after Baby Joe had been put to bed, and the rest of the
family had gathered in the lounge.

'Now then, Ed,' Mr Englefield began, eyeing his small,
subdued son. 'You're worried about this school magazine
of yours, aren't you?'

'Of course he is, Dad,' Karen said wearily. 'Everyone knows that. The thing is, he's only got a week left in which to dig up a fantastic story that all the kids will want to read.'

'Or the *Bugle* will be scrapped,' sighed Ed.

'Well, *surely* we can come up with something between us,' said Mr Englefield. He glanced at his wife, who had moved to the dining table. 'What do *you* think, Mother?'

'Er, just a minute, George. I'm trying to find the tips of Copenhagen's ears.'

'The tips of *what*?'

'Ah, there they are!' With a triumphant cry, Mrs Englefield snatched up a piece of jig-saw, and inserted it in the half-completed, 'Kingsize' puzzle that sprawled across the table. Completing kingsize jig-saw puzzles,

67

depicting scenes from famous historical battles, was her favourite form of relaxation. Especially scenes from the Battle of Waterloo.

'He didn't look right without ears,' she said, looking up, and beaming at the room in general. 'Copenhagen was the Duke of Wellington's horse, you know!'

'Thanks for the history lesson, dear,' Mr Englefield said patiently. 'Now perhaps you'll concentrate on the issue at hand; which is finding a . . . a . . .'

'Scoop,' said Karen.

'A scoop for Ed's school magazine!'

'I've been concentrating on it for some time, actually,' said Mrs Englefield, sorting through the puzzle pieces again. 'And *I* think he ought to go and have a chat with that Norman Clegg fellow.'

No one said anything for a moment. So Mrs Englefield went on, 'You know, Ed . . . the footballer. The one that's just been transported to Chiverton Athletic.'

'You mean "transferred", Mum,' said Ed. 'And I *did* think about interviewing him for the *Bugle*, but—'

'He dropped the idea,' interrupted Mr Englefield. 'And I should *think* so! That man is all mouth and football boots. He's been sent off the field more times than I've had hot dinners! It's no wonder they call him the "Cruncher"!'

It was certainly true that Norman 'Cruncher' Clegg had an explosive temper, and a very high opinion of himself. In the opinion of the experts, it was Norman's flair for 'crunching' the opposition which had prevented him from scaling football's dizziest heights, and winning a place in the England team.

But Chiverton Athletic, the local professional football team, were desperate. Having finished in the bottom half of the Fourth Division the previous seven seasons, they badly needed the excitement and glamour that a famous player would generate. A 'character' who would appeal to the local football fans, and bring them flocking back to the Athletic's deserted terraces.

'Clegg's famous, all right,' snorted Mr Englefield. 'He's famous for kicking people over the touchline!'

'That may be so, dear,' said Mrs Englefield calmly, adding another piece to her puzzle, 'but Chiverton were still prepared to buy him from another club for *fifty thousand pounds!* I hear they almost went out of business, trying to raise the money.'

'Serves 'em right if they do,' snorted her husband. 'They only managed to buy Clegg because all the other clubs wouldn't touch him with a barge pole. If I was Ed, I'd forget all about him!'

'I already have, Dad,' said Ed. 'I mean, the *Chronicle* is bound to do a big feature on Clegg, so why should anyone want to read the same old stuff in the school mag?'

'I suppose not,' mused Karen, scratching her chin. 'But what if you gave the article a different "slant", as you newspaper people say? For instance, I'll bet the kids at school would love to know how Norman Clegg was discovered!'

'They probably found him under a stone!' muttered Mr Englefield.

'Or what it's really like to be a professional footballer,' Karen went on.

'You mean . . . a sort of Glimpse behind the Scenes?' Ed said thoughtfully. He was beginning to sense the possibilities. 'The inside story of football . . . straight from the mouth of Norman Clegg!'

'That's right, darling,' said Mrs Englefield. 'I'm sure

it'll be much more interesting than all that routine stuff they print in the *Chronicle*.'

'You could be right, Mum.' Ed was pacing up and down excitedly, wondering where he had put his note-book. 'I might even persuade him to visit the school, and give a lecture to the senior players. Perhaps hold a few practice sessions!'

'Never in a thousand years,' said Mr Englefield. 'I mean, *think* about it, son! There'll be so many people fussing around Norman Clegg, the *last* thing he'll want to do is talk to editors of school magazines!'

Ed knew that his father was trying to spare him from further disappointment. But nothing could dampen his enthusiasm now. On the way home from school the fol-lowing afternoon, he stopped at the first public telephone kiosk, dialled the number of the *Chiverton Chronicle*, and asked to speak to the Editor.

'The editor's busy at the moment, sir,' the girl on the switchboard told him. 'Is there anyone else who can help you?'

'I expect so, miss,' said Ed politely. He had wedged his notebook under his chin, because the bit of shelf on which the telephone rested was too high for making notes. 'Y'see, I'm trying to find out when Norman Clegg will be arriving at Chiverton Athletic football club.'

There was a long silence, followed by a few clicks. 'I'm afraid the sports section is engaged, sir. I'll put you through to Features.'

Another click. And a buzz. Then, through a sudden pandemonium of clacking typewriters, a voice said crisply, 'Features here! Fenton Broadway speaking!'

Ed almost dropped the telephone. Fenton Broadway –

the leading feature writer for the *Chiverton Chronicle*!
Ed regarded him as a sort of rival. He had a sudden vision
of the round, owl-like, heavy-jowled face that adorned
every single one of Broadway's articles. A smug,
pompous sort of face . . .

'Broadway here!' Who's speaking?' The journalist's
voice, a trifle impatient now, crackled into Ed's thoughts.
'Hello! *Hello, Hello!*'

'Hello,' said Ed.

'Hello? Look, who *is* this? Who's there?'

'My name's Ed, Mr Broadway . . . I mean, Englefield.
I'm telephoning about Norman Clegg. You know – the
footballer!'

The telephone hissed with suspicious silence. Then Ed
heard a lot of muttering and whispering at the other end
of the line, before Broadway said cautiously, 'Er, what about
Norman Clegg? Are you from one of the news agencies?'

'Oh, no, Mr Broadway, I'm from the *Bugle*!'

'The *Bugle*, eh?' Fenton Broadway's voice brightened
considerably. 'Well, why didn't you say so, old chap!
Now, don't tell me. Let me guess! Englefield . . .
Englefield . . .' A pause, then, 'You're not with the *Manchester Bugle*, are you?'

'No.'

'That's strange. I'm sure I knew an Englefield on the
Manchester Bugle. The *Liverpool Bugle*, then.'

'Nope.'

'Well, WHAT *Bugle* are you with, then?' Broadway's
voice was becoming impatient again. Irritated, in fact.
'The *Sheffield Bugle?* Exeter? Northampton?'

'It's the *Baker Street School Bugle*, actually,' said Ed.

'The Baker Street Sch – Look, what *is* this? Some kind
of hoax? Who *are* you?'

'Edward Englefield, Mr Broadway. I'm the editor of our school magazine, y'see, and—'

'Why, you stupid little idiot!' Ed winced as Broadway's voice thundered into his ear. 'How dare you pester me on the 'phone while I'm in the middle of an important piece! If you ever try anything like this again, I'll find out where you live and report you to your parents, is that clear? NOW GET OFF THE LINE!'

Ed winced again as the telephone slammed down at the other end of the line. I must have caught Mr Broadway on one of his busy days, he thought, as he left the kiosk, hardly noticing the large, glaring woman who had been stamping up and down outside. For Ed had suddenly realised that there had been no need to telephone the *Chronicle* at all! Fancy forgetting that Johnny Rackham's brother, Tony, was also a professional footballer with Chiverton Athletic! He'd be bound to know when Norman Clegg was due to arrive.

In fact it was Tony Rackham who answered the door, when Ed called at Johnny's house, twenty minutes later.

The young professional, who was usually ready for a chat or a joke, paused only to let Ed into the house, before trailing despondently back upstairs to his room, looking utterly fed up.

'It's this Cruncher Clegg business that's upset him,' Johnny explained. 'Tony was hoping to make the first team, this season. But now that Chiverton have bought Clegg, he's got no chance. They both play in the same position, see – on the right flank, behind the strikers.'

'So Tony will be stuck in the reserves again?' Ed shook his head sympathetically. He felt a little guilty about bothering the Rackhams at such a time. But if he was going to save the *Bugle* there could be no room for sentiment. 'I, er ... don't suppose Tony's feeling in the mood to tell me about Clegg, then?' Ed went on. 'About when he's arriving, I mean.'

'There's no need to ask our kid,' Johnny said. 'He's already told me. The club's rolling out the red carpet for the Cruncher at about one o'clock tomorrow afternoon!'

Ed didn't even tell Cyril North what he was going to do during the school lunch break the following day. Or where he was going. If he was going to get anywhere with Norman Clegg, he couldn't afford to have Cyril flitting around like a nervous budgie.

At precisely ten minutes to one, Ed left his bike in the big public car-park adjoining Chiverton football stadium, and set off for the main entrance. As usual, pens, pencils, press cards and notebook were all in their proper places, although Ed had taken the precaution of hiding his camera under his left armpit.

He had no particular plan of action in mind, apart from getting as close to Norman Clegg as possible, which meant sneaking through the huge crowd of reporters, photographers, and club officials that Ed saw spilling across the pavement ahead of him, almost blocking the narrow street. They were all chattering excitedly, and looking expectantly up the street, as Ed eased himself into the forest of bodies. He had almost reached the front of the crowd, when someone yelled, 'This looks like the car now! He's coming!'

The crowd jostled and swayed, trapping Ed in a seething, crushing mass of tweed jackets, and two-piece suits. 'Ouch!' yelped a reporter, as Ed's camera, dislodged in the confusion, thumped down on to his foot. 'Hey! Someone's dropped a camera!'

Before Ed could stop him, the man picked up the

camera, and peered at the neatly printed label which was stuck to the back of it.

'Belongs to someone called "Englefield",' the reporter called out, 'of the *Baker Street Bugle*!'

'Did you say ENGLEFIELD?'

The second voice was horribly familiar to Ed. He had heard it the day before, on the other end of a telephone line. In the flesh, and wearing a dark blue blazer and spotty bow tie, Fenton Broadway looked even more like a furious, black-browed owl. Before Ed could dart away, one of the owl's chubby talons fastened on his collar.

'So YOU are the little pest who goes around telephoning newspaper offices, pretending to be a reporter!'

'I *am* a reporter, Mr Broadway, honest,' Ed said breathlessly. 'I'm writing a football feature for the *Bugle*.'

'Oh, yes? Well, here's a sample headline for you; GRUBBY LITTLE NUISANCE FEELS THE POWER OF BROADWAY'S RIGHT FOOT!'

Something collided with the seat of Ed's grey flannel trousers, sending him reeling into a nest of dustbins which stood outside the players' entrance. He was still trying to disentangle himself when a car drew up, and out climbed a tall, dark, lean-jawed figure, resplendent in rakish jacket, and an open-necked, red silk shirt. As photographers rushed forward, Norman Clegg hitched up his velvet, flared slacks like a visiting gunfighter, smoothed his well-shampooed, fashionably styled hair, and leered at the clicking cameras.

Ed groaned inwardly. The Cruncher had come to town – all fifty-thousand-pounds-worth of him – and here was the Editor of the *Bugle*, struggling to free himself from a stack of dustbins.

'Welcome to Chiverton, Norman,' he heard Fenton

Broadway boom. Cameras phutted and clicked again as the Chiverton Manager stepped forward, and shook hands with his new star. Then everyone and everything closed around Clegg, and swept him on into the stadium. Out of sight . . . Out of reach . . .

For the moment, anyway, thought Ed, dusting himself down as best he could. Picking up his camera, he eyed the club official who now stood guard at the closed doors of the main entrance, and began to trudge off back towards the car park. He wasn't going to give up as easily as this. It was rumoured that Chiverton Athletic had even presented Norman Clegg with a house, as part of the transfer agreement. If Ed could find out where it was situated, he could call on the Cruncher at a later date, and interview him in peace and quiet.

As he re-entered the car park Ed noticed a small door which seemed to be a rear exit from one end of the main grandstand. No harm in finding out where it led to. It was sort of trespassing, Ed had to admit. But his feature on Clegg was bound to create a blaze of publicity for the club, and all he wanted to do was question one of the other players, or perhaps a groundsman.

To his relief, the door was unlocked. Beyond it a corridor of chipped, green-painted brick walls stretched away into the quiet shadows, merging with a little maze of other corridors, and rooms. Rooms marked 'Boot Store', 'Visitors Dressing-room', and 'Showers'. And then, just round a bend, to Ed's left, another door marked 'Home Dressing-room'.

It was almost wide open. And there, completely and utterly alone, stood Cruncher Clegg! He had changed into a smart, navy-blue tracksuit, and training boots, and was standing in front of a mirror, carefully brushing his hair, and smirking at himself, as if preparing for an audience at Buckingham Palace.

Suddenly, as if conscious of Ed's bulging eyes upon him, the Cruncher whipped round, glared, and snapped, 'All right, what's yer game then, kid?' If you're looking for my autograph—'

'Oh, no, Mr Clegg,' Ed blurted, reaching hastily for a press card. 'I'm not after your autograph. I mean, I'd love your autograph. But I'm a reporter, actually, representing the *Bugle*!'

'A reporter?' Norman Clegg blinked at the dusty, dishevelled dwarf that confronted him. At the battered camera, slung around the dwarf's neck. 'Get off! You're 'avin' me on!' the Hope of Chiverton said.

'No, honest, Mr Clegg! I'm here on behalf of our school magazine, y'see, and—' Ed gabbled on, desperate to capture the Cruncher's attention, before someone arrived to whisk him away again. He ended his breathless little speech by thrusting a crumpled press card into the footballer's hand.

Norman Clegg squinted at the card, like a large, short-sighted child who was still learning to read. 'Edward Englefield! Editor, feature writer, an' Chief Staff Reporter of the – *Baker Street Bugle?*'

He peered down at Ed over the top of the card. 'You're a bit small to 'andle all that lot, ain't yer?' Tossing the press card over his shoulder, the Cruncher turned back to the mirror. 'Anyway, why should I bother about a kids' magazine? That fat geezer from the *Chronicle* is gonna do a big spread on me. And they're paying me for it, too!'

'Ah, but it's only *adults* that read the *Chronicle*,' Ed said quickly. 'If you do an interview for the *Bugle* you'll be, er

. . . reaching out to the footballers of the future! Adults don't care much about Chiverton Athletic, Mr Clegg, but the kids at our school went mad when they heard you were coming!'

'They did, eh?'

'Yes,' Ed plunged on. 'They . . . they're all doing part-time jobs to raise money to come an' watch you! You're their inspiration, Mr Clegg! They're dying to know all about you. What your favourite food is . . .'

'Prawn curry an' chips, mate. You can't beat a nice plate o' Prawn curry an' chips!'

'. . . And how you were discovered! Or what it's like to play for some of the most famous football clubs in England!'

'Now *that's* a story in itself, that is! You wouldn't believe some of the things that go on!' Clegg stopped brushing his hair, and glanced narrowly at Ed. 'Er . . . what's the circulation of this *Bugle*, then?'

'Well,' said Ed, taking a deep breath. 'There's about five hundred kids at our school who are just crackers about football!'

'Five hundred, eh?' The Cruncher began to pace up and down, staring thoughtfully into space. 'That's five hundred familes, really, en it? An' I expect their dads an' brothers will read the article, too. Yeah, it might be a giggle! I might even come along to the school, an' hold a football surgery!'

'Or a clinic,' prompted Ed. 'Give a demonstration of your incredible skills.'

'All right!' The Cruncher smacked a fist into the palm of his other hand. 'I'll do it!' He swung round, and glared at Ed. 'But if anyone wants me autograph, it'll cost 'em ten pence. *Fifty* pence for photographs. An' that's cheap,

I'm tellin' yer! My agent would go potty if he found out I was doing 'em as cheap as that!'

Ed hadn't reckoned on being charged for autographs. But he could worry about that later. All that mattered was that he was being granted an interview. A real live interview at long last!

He scribbled page after page as the Cruncher marched up and down, and rambled on and on. Ed couldn't even get a word in, especially when Clegg got round to the painful subject of *not* being picked to play for England, '... just because I got sent off for crocking one of the England manager's blue-eyed boys,' he snarled. 'All that stuff in the papers about having to have seven stitches in his leg was a load of old rubbish! I just grazed 'im wiv me studs, that's all! And then he goes tellin' tales about me to the England boss. Put the knife in, he did. Cor, I

was as sick as a parrot when I heard I wasn't in the squad!
Sick as a perishin' parrot ...' And so on. Much in the
same vein. Players seemed to have been going behind
Clegg's back at every club he had played for. By the time
the Cruncher launched into a description of his famous
Horizontal Mid-air Bicycle Kick, Ed was becoming a
little worried. He would have to re-write the whole interview. Or at least, tone it down a little. Far from inspiring
the readers of the *Bugle*, it was likely to put them off
football for good. It was almost a relief when Clegg's
voice suddenly trailed into silence.

'Well, that's it,' the Cruncher said after a moment,
turning back to the mirror, and giving his hair a pat or
two. 'The *true* story of Norman Clegg. I suppose you'll be
wanting a photograph now?'

'If you don't mind, Mr Clegg,' said Ed, 'could you take
off your tracksuit, please? Then I can get a shot of you
wearing Chiverton's colours—'

'OH, NO YOU WON'T!'

The angry, incredulous voice seemed to explode in Ed's
ears. He didn't have to look round to realise that the
chubby hand which fell on his shoulder belonged to
Fenton Broadway. 'It's just as well I came to find out what
was keeping you, Norman! Been filling you up with a lot
of nonsense about magazines, and reporters, has he?'

'It ... it isn't nonsense,' gasped Ed, struggling in Broadway's grip. 'This is a proper interview. Mr Clegg *agreed*
to let me interview him!'

'That's right,' growled the Cruncher. 'He reckoned the
article would be read by five hundred kids, and I'd get ten
pence for every autograph.'

'HAW!' snorted Fenton Broadway contemptuously.
'Let me assure you, my dear Norman, it was just a trick to

impress you. Even if there *is* a school rag called the *Bugle*, and even if this little toad *is* the editor – which I doubt – you wouldn't get a penny out of it!'

'But he even had a press card,' muttered Norman Clegg, peering at the floor. 'He showed it to me.' It was all getting a bit beyond him. What kind of a crummy town had he landed up in this time? Kids pretending to be reporters! 'Do you mean to say,' he said incredulously, 'that I've been tellin' him all that stuff about me for nothing?'

'I'm afraid so, Norman!' Tossing Ed aside like an unwanted football programme, Fenton Broadway grabbed the Cruncher's arm, and began to bustle him out into the corridor. 'The only press people you need to worry about are waiting for you on the pitch, right now. We're going to do the *lot*, Norman. Action shots. Profiles. A two-page spread in the *Chronicle*, just as I promised!'

'Great!' said the Cruncher.

'And as for *you*, my lad . . .' Broadway threw a parting glare at Ed. 'You'd better get out of this stadium the same way you came in! But you haven't heard the last of this! Oh, no! First thing tomorrow I'm going round to that school of yours to see your headmaster! And *then* you'll be for it!'

'That's the stuff, Fenton,' chuckled Norman Clegg, as they moved off. 'You tell 'im!'

But the journalist's threat hadn't worried Ed in the least. In fact, as the two men vanished around a bend in the corridor, all the weeks of pent-up frustration – all the days of shattered hopes and interfering adults – were beginning to ignite a small, but ominous spark of indignation within the editor of the *Baker Street Bugle* . . .

Out on the pitch, a moment later, the crowd of press

people jostled for position again as fifty-thousand-pounds-worth of footballer emerged from the players' tunnel with Fenton Broadway.

'Everything all right, Norman?' the Chiverton Manager called out anxiously.

'You bet, Boss. Just some kid making a nuisance of himself.'

Stripping off his tracksuit, the Cruncher embarked on a whirlwind limbering-up routine, which included a series of vicious-looking high kicks.

'Old Fenton wants to get some shots of the old Horizontal Mid-air Bicycle Kick!' he yelled, making a sudden, head-down sprint through a group of photographers.

'Well, okay, Norman. But take it easy,' said the Chiverton Manager, dabbing at his forehead with a tissue. He broke out in a cold sweat every time he thought of that colossal transfer fee. It was colossal for Chiverton Athletic, anyway. His last, fervent prayer, before falling asleep at night, was that Norman Clegg would be worth it. It was vital that the Athletic made a good start to the season, and recaptured some of those missing fans.

'I'm sure that the arrival of Norman Clegg will mark a turning point in the fortunes of Chiverton Athletic football club,' Fenton Broadway was booming, as if he had read the manager's thoughts.

'Hey, I like it! I like it!' cried Norman. 'You've certainly got a way wiv words, Fenton.' Taking off in a tremendous leap, the Cruncher rolled his body in mid-air, legs flailing like giant scissors as he lashed out at an imaginary ball. A spectacular demonstration of the deadly Horizontal Mid-air Bicycle Kick!

'Fantastic!' breathed Fenton Broadway. 'Now I'd like

you to do it again, Norman using a football this time.
The real thing, eh?'

'Yeah! Ready when you are, tiger!'

Broadway bustled around importantly, getting everyone into position. He stationed the Chiverton Manager,
armed with a football, on the edge of the penalty area of
one of the goals and instructed him to toss the ball
towards the Hope of Chiverton, as soon as the photographers were ready.

'An' then I give it the works,' grinned the Cruncher.
'One, two, an' SMACK in the old onion-bag!'

'That's the stuff, Norman,' beamed Fenton Broadway.

'Don't overdo it, lad,' pleaded the Chiverton Manager.

As Norman Clegg fell into a watchful crouch, and the
photographers knelt and aimed their cameras, no one saw
the mop of tousled, reddish hair that began to rise up
from behind the barrier, just to one side of the goal.

It was Ed, his eye firmly glued to the viewfinder of his
own, battered box camera. Without quite knowing how,
he had found his way – via a labyrinth of passages and
doors – on to the concrete terracing at one end of the
ground. The right end, as it turned out. And now Ed's
blood was up. Whatever the outcome, he was going to
complete at least one assignment for the *Bugle*. And he
might never get a better chance to photograph Cruncher
Clegg.

'Let's get weaving,' yelled Norman impatiently. 'I'll
take root in a minute!'

Ed rose a little higher, searching for a better angle. Just
a slight, furtive movement. But Fenton Broadway's beady
eyes spotted it.

'I don't believe it – I *don't*! IT'S THAT CONFOUN-
DED KID AGAIN!' he roared, and went galloping across

the pitch ... just as the Chiverton Manager tossed the ball to Norman Clegg, and Norman heaved himself into the air. His view blocked by Fenton Broadway's lumbering figure, Clegg completely missed the ball, which smacked against his nose, causing him to lose his balance in mid-air. Then ... THWOMMMPF! the Cruncher flopped down on the penalty spot like a helpless, blue-and-white scarecrow.

'EEEAAAAAARGH!'

Led by the Chiverton Manager, officials and reporters rushed towards fifty-thousand-pound-worth of writhing, howling footballer. Fresh howls went up as the club's trainer poked and prodded at one of the Cruncher's legs.

'It's his right knee, Boss,' the trainer said at last, break-ing the horrified hush which had fallen. 'Must have twisted it as he fell.'

'Oh, n-no!' Like a man who has just seen a ghost, the Chiverton Manager lurched to his feet, and turned towards Fenton Broadway. 'Of all the stupid, clumsy, l-lumbering great fatheads! You . . . you ran straight between us! Norman didn't stand a chance!'

'But I . . . I—'

'He'll probably miss half the season now! I've a good mind to sue the *Chronicle* for damages!'

'Don't blame me,' bleated Fenton Broadway, flapping his arms like a frantic owl. 'Blame that kid! I . . . I was trying to stop him from taking a photograph of Norman!'

'Kid? *What* kid?'

'The one that's been pestering Norman all day! He's over there . . . behind the barrier!' The plump journalist pointed desperately towards the goal. But now there was no sign of the kid who had been 'pestering' Norman Clegg.

The Editor of the *Bugle* had already decided that it was time he collected his bike from the stadium car park . . .

As Mrs Englefield – who was a mine of mysterious sayings – often said, 'It's an ill wind that blows nobody any good', which meant that the injury to Norman Clegg compelled his manager to draft Tony Rackham into Chiverton's first team.

Tony's delighted brother, Johnny, insisted on dragging Ed along to the Athletic's first match of the season, against Railford Town, the following Saturday. And when Tony scored the goal that gave Chiverton an unbeatable, three-nil lead, late in the game, even Ed joined in the wild tumult of cheering.

'You'll have to write an article about our kid now, Ed,' whooped Johnny, as they danced triumphantly on the terraces – the same terraces where Ed had witnessed the downfall of Norman 'Cruncher' Clegg.

Ed had torn up his notes on Clegg as soon as he had got home. Not even the most fanatical soccer fan would want to read about a footballer who had crocked himself doing a Horizontal Mid-air Bicycle Kick. There was always Tony Rackham, of course, but . . .

'Come on, our kid,' yelled Johnny. 'Let's have another one!'

'Yeah, make it four!' yelled Ed. He was doing his best to share Johnny Rackham's enthusiasm. Perhaps in a few years time, if Johnny's brother became good enough to play for England, he'd be worth writing about. But by then the *Baker Street Bugle* might have ceased to exist.

Fate takes a hand

Rain gusted from the slate-grey sky. A thin, spiteful sort of rain, driven by a chilly, north-easterly wind that snatched and tugged at the hood of Ed's anorak, as he cycled laboriously through the narrow streets of Chiverton. He bent lower over his handlebars, almost wishing that the journey would never end — that he would never arrive at Baker Street School, where the last edition of the *Bugle* was waiting to be produced.

Ed was so certain that it *would* be the last issue, he hadn't even called for Cyril. A torrent of well-meaning advice and sympathy was the last thing he wanted on this cheerless morning.

Thankfully, his father had understood. 'Never mind, lad,' Mr Englefield had said, casually dropping a tenpence piece into the breast-pocket of Ed's shirt. 'That school magazine was just cramping your style. You'll be a famous Fleet Street editor one day, mark my words.'

But Ed couldn't be consoled; not even by his favourite breakfast of beefburger and spaghetti rings in tomato sauce, lovingly cooked by Mrs Englefield. He had hardly touched the meal, so his mother had made a mountain of sandwiches, and stuffed them into his satchel. What with

the wind and the rain, and the weight of the sandwiches, Ed was feeling quite exhausted as he turned at last through the school gates, and almost fell into the bicycle sheds.

'MORNING, ENGLEFIELD!'

It was Mr Gillard, bearing down on him, bent against the rain. The Assistant Headmaster's spectacles were so steamed up with condensation, he almost collided with the side of the shed. He recoiled, and boomed, 'Today's the day, eh? I'm really looking forward to reading this month's edition of the *Bugle*! Heard it might contain an interview with a famous film actress, or something...'

'You mean, Fiona Redburn, sir? Well, as a matter of fact—'

'And a touching story about an old lady and her parrot! Wasn't it *you* that helped to find a home for it—'

'Er, not exactly, sir. Y'see—'

'Fantastic stuff! Oh, yes indeed! I can see you took my advice to heart, lad!' Lifting his steamed-up specs an inch or two to find out where he was, Mr Gillard located the main school entrance, and set course for it like a wind-racked galleon. 'Make sure you let me have the first copy, Englefield,' he roared back. 'With all that excitement and drama packed into every page, the *Bugle* is bound to be in big demand!'

It'll be in demand, all right, thought Ed. For wrapping fish-and-chips! He had, in fact, been toying with the idea of admitting to Mr Gillard that all his interviews had drawn a blank, and that it wasn't really worth publishing the *Bugle* this month. Now, to make things worse, the Assistant Head was obviously expecting a colossal literary triumph.

'Why don't you have a "boom"?' suggested Cyril, during morning break.

'A "boom"?' said Ed, not really listening. Although the rain had stopped, the wind was still charging about, scattering ripples across the puddles in the playground.

'*You* know,' Cyril went on, 'like they do in the comics. A BOOM! Give away a free gift with every copy!'

'*Free gift?*' Ed stared at his friend, incredulously.

'YOU know! Something useful. Like paper-clips, or . . . or second-hand biros. You've got loads of 'em in your office!'

'Or maybe we could raffle your old football boots,' Ed said drily.

Cyril shook his head doubtfully. 'Dunno about that. I mean, you could only sell tickets to the kids who take my size, and—'

'Yeah, you're right, Northy. It might get a bit complicated,' Ed said, offering Cyril a cheese-and-pickle sandwich. Northy's ideas were pretty daft at times, but at least he was trying. 'We'd better forget about booms, and free gifts. But not to worry. I expect I'll think of something.'

But the only thought that occurred to Ed, as he headed for the *Bugle*'s office at lunch-time, was that the sooner he got it all over with, the better.

He had to squeeze into the little room. Someone had crammed his trestle table and duplicator into a corner, and dumped a fresh pile of sports equipment in the middle of the floor. As if the *Bugle* had already been written off. Given a hasty, and untidy burial.

Clearing a small space in the corner, Ed embarked on the task of printing the last fifty copies. He had carefully drafted the magazine's contents on to several sheets of stencil paper the previous evening, so now all he had to do was feed them into the duplicator.

Ed's spirits plunged a little lower as he made a final check on the various features. The usual sports results and school gossip. An article on local brass-rubbings, written by Mr Forbes. A short story about a naughty hedgehog, contributed by Mrs Goodenough. And a fiery piece by Valerie Pigden, calling for an end to homework.

Lastly, almost as an afterthought, there was Ed's new horoscope feature. Jupiter in the Sign of Gemini. Omens and Lucky Numbers. It wasn't exactly a collection of Searing Human Dramas, to say the least!

As he began to turn the handle of the duplicator, and the first damp pages slid from the rollers, Ed thought

ruefully that he didn't need a horoscope to forecast the future of the *Bugle*...

Ed took up his usual position near the main gates immediately after school. Pestering every pupil that passed, he managed to sell fourteen copies of the *Bugle*. An increase of three copies over the previous month's sales. But that was only because Valerie Pigden held a short 'demo' in support of her article, and bullied three of her cronies into reading it.

'It's no use, Northy,' Ed said to Cyril, who had come along to help out. 'They're just not interested in brass-rubbings, and naughty hedgehogs.'

'We haven't tried the playing fields yet,' Cyril said hopefully. 'The Under-15 girls have got a hockey match against Grovelands. Your Karen's playing. We might be able to sell a few copies in the crowd.'

'It's just a girls' hockey match, Cyril, not the FA Cup

Final. But if you think it's worth a try . . .' Ed thrust a few copies of the *Bugle* into Cyril's hands, '. . . you go ahead and try. I'm going home.'

'All right, go on, then,' cried Cyril, as Ed trudged away. 'But I . . . I bet I sell 'em! I mean, your Karen's bound to buy one, for a start!'

In fact Karen Englefield had already bought a copy of the *Bugle*, out of sheer loyalty to Ed. And over in the hockey team's dressing-room, she was doing her best to persuade her team-mates to follow suit.

'You want to know what's going on in school, don't you?' Karen was saying, waving the *Bugle* around desperately. 'It's got articles, short stories. And . . . and a smashing new *horoscope* feature!'

'Don't believe in 'em,' said one of the girls, too busy lacing her boots to heed Karen's sales talk.

'You would if you followed them,' insisted Karen. 'Why, I bet if I read out one, it would seem completely fantastic. Let's try someone, and see.' She looked round the dressing-room. 'What's yours, Erica?'

Erica Roberts, already changed, sat in the corner of the room, wrapped in her own, nervous thoughts.

'What's my what?'

'Your horoscope sign, twit!'

'Dunno.'

'Well, what's your date of birth, then?'

'Er . . . twenty-seventh of May,' Erica muttered.

'Twenty-seventh of May . . .' Karen consulted the list of horoscopes. 'That means you're a Gemini.' Her voice becoming hoarse with excitement, she read on, 'YOUR PLANETARY ASPECTS HAVE NEVER BEEN MORE FAVOURABLE. ALL YOU NEED IS THE

93

COURAGE TO STRIKE OUT, AND YOU ARE BOUND TO ACHIEVE YOUR GOAL. THE LETTER "B" IS SIGNIFICANT. LUCKY NUMBER 3!'

'What about *that* then?' Karen gasped, looking up from her copy of the *Bugle*. But Erica had already gone, filing out on to the pitch with the rest of the team.

She hadn't even heard that her lucky number was three, because Erica's thoughts were preoccupied with a much more serious issue – her current loss of form. The team's right inner forward, she hadn't scored a single goal in the school's last four games, and Erica knew that she would be dropped from the team if she failed to find the net against Grovelands.

During the opening minutes of the match it was the same old story. All her passes went astray, and she missed two good chances. Then, making a determined foray down the right, Karen whipped the ball into the middle. It glanced off an opponent's stick, and rolled towards Erica. Normally, Erica would have trapped the ball, and looked round for someone to pass to. But it was all or nothing now. And surely her luck couldn't get any worse!

Closing her eyes, she unleashed a mighty, desperate swipe. There was a sharp crack, followed by a dull thud ... and then a triumphant roar exploded from the Baker Street Supporters.

'GOAL!'

Through a haze of relief and joy, Erica saw the crestfallen Grovelands' goalkeeper sitting on her rump. The ball was behind her, nestling snugly in the back of the net.

'You SEE!' Karen Englefield screamed, almost leaping on to Erica's back. 'I TOLD you there was something in it! It told you to STRIKE OUT, and you DID! And you SCORED!'

Erica hadn't the faintest idea what Karen was going on about. All she knew was that it had been a lucky shot, probably helped on its way by the wind, which was still fairly strong. Now, as the game continued, she seemed to become part of the wind, rotating around the pitch in a series of breath-taking dribbles. Opponent after opponent was left floundering in her wake. A last side-step, and the Grovelands goal, with its trembling occupant, yawned at Erica's mercy. Somewhere behind her, Karen was yelling, 'SHOOT, ERICA! HIT IT! GO FOR THE FLIPPIN' GOAL!'

Karen was still yelling as she arrived home, about ten minutes after the hockey match had ended. Pounding up the stairs, she began to hammer on the door of Ed's room, which was locked from the inside.

'Ed,' she gasped, 'ED! You'll never believe what's happened! It came true — every word of it!'

'What did?'

'Erica Roberts' horoscope!'

'Good for her,' said Ed. He was lying on his bed, trapped under the sprawling bulk of Charles the Fourth. Sensing that his master wasn't in the best of spirits, the huge boxer had sneaked upstairs to console him, but had merely succeeded in making Ed's left leg go numb.

Karen pounded on the door again. 'Ed, what are you doing? For pete's sake, open this door!'

'What for?'

'So's I can tell you about Erica Roberts!'

'Tell me from there. I'm trying to read.'

'Read your own magazine, then! It told Erica Roberts that she would achieve her goal if she struck out fearlessly! And that her lucky number was three! And it WAS! She scored a HAT-TRICK, Ed!'

'It's about time, so I hear,' Ed said absently, turning back to his book. It was entitled. *The Secrets of Successful Writing*. Ed was hoping that it might tell him where he had gone wrong with the *Bugle*.

'For the last time, Ed Englefield, are you going to open this door?'

'NO HE'S NOT, KAREN! Now come down here, this minute, and leave him alone!'

Ed sighed with relief as he heard his mother's voice, calling from the hall.

'But, Mum . . .' Karen's footsteps retreated reluctantly down the stairs. 'I'm trying to tell him about Erica Roberts' horoscope!'

'You can tell him in the morning, darling. Ed's probably feeling a bit upset because his *Bugle*'s gone wrong again. It'll do him good to have an early night . . .' As their voices faded into the kitchen, Ed thought vaguely about Erica Roberts' hat-trick. Funny how it should tie in with her horoscope. But it was just a coincidence, of course. And it would take more than a coincidence to save the *Bugle* . . .

Mr Gillard was thinking much the same thing, as he sat on the top deck of a packed, slow-moving No. 19 bus to Chiverton Park, thumbing morosely through his personal copy of the *Bugle*. Young Englefield had let him down. Let him down badly. This month's issue was about as exciting as a Party Political Broadcast.

But at that particular moment, not even a thousand Searing Human Dramas could have dispersed the cloud of utter despair which had settled over the Assistant Headmaster.

It was Mrs Gillard who had started it all. She had telephoned him in mid-afternoon, with the latest report on the Gillards' ailing car, which had recently broken down for the umpteenth time. According to the garage where the infernal vehicle now resided, it was going to need a new gear-box, three new tyres, and goodness knows what done to the Front Suspension Cross-member, whatever *that* was. In short . . . a repair bill of nearly two hundred pounds.

Mrs Gillard had ended by informing him that she was unable to leave the house, because one of her Severe Headaches had come on. So Mr Gillard would have to do the shopping on his way home from school.

The Assistant Headmaster groaned, and rubbed miserably at his large lumpy nose. That wretched car had been a constant strain on his bank balance. He hadn't a hope of raising fifty pounds, let alone two hundred. In the circumstances, Englefield's new horoscope feature seemed quite ludicrous. Especially the horoscope relating to his own Zodiac sign, which was Leo. To the utter amazement of nearby passengers, Mr Gillard began to read it aloud in a bitter, grating voice:

'RECENT SET-BACKS ARE ABOUT TO DISAPPEAR. EVERYTHING IS SET FAIR, AND YOU ARE DUE FOR A FANTASTIC SURPRISE, AS YOU CROSS THE THRESHOLD OF FATE. THE INFLUENCE OF JUPITER WILL PROD YOU INTO ACTION, ENABLING YOU TO GRASP THESE GOLDEN OPPORTUNITIES WITH BOTH HANDS!'

Mr Gillard broke off as the bus shuddered to a halt. Glancing from a window, he saw, to his horror, that they

were on the outskirts of Chiverton. Thanks to that con-
founded horoscope, he had missed his stop, and passed
through the town centre. As he struggled from his seat,
plunged down the stairs, and almost fell off the bus, he
noticed that the few shops in the area were in the process
of closing. All except Fair-Line Stores, a huge supermarket which had opened a few months ago.

Mr Gillard *hated* supermarkets. All those beastly wire
trolleys, coming at you from every angle. And he could
never remember where they kept the tea-bags. But he'd
rather face the perils of a supermarket, than go home to
Mrs Gillard empty handed.

Pausing only to stuff his copy of the *Bugle* into a litter-
bin, Mr Gillard squared his shoulders, and joined a little
group of shoppers who were about to enter the store. As
he passed through the big, glass swing doors, someone
shouted, *'That's the one! The chap with the glasses!'* and a
heavy hand fell on his shoulder.

For a horrible moment Mr Gillard thought he was
being arrested for shop-lifting. 'I ... I haven't stolen
anything, honest!' he gasped at the crisp, young
man who had grabbed him. 'I ... I'm the Assistant
Headmaster at Baker Street School, and I've only just
arrived!'

'Of *course* you have, sir,' beamed the young man, who
was obviously the manager. 'In fact, you're the
MILLIONTH customer to pass across the threshold of
this store, since it was opened.' The young man's voice
rose to a dramatic shout. 'Which means that you have
won our fantastic Golden Prize! A week's holiday for
two on the Costa Brava, or THREE HUNDRED AND
FIFTY POUNDS IN CASH!'

Mr Gillard just stood there, mouth hanging open, as

shop assistants cheered and clapped, and a photographer sprang forward to take a photograph of the Assistant Head shaking hands with the manager. Three hundred and fifty pounds! It would be enough to pay for the repairs to the car, plus a little left over.

'I'll t-take the money,' gasped Mr Gillard.

'All in good time, sir,' the store manager beamed, whisking Mr Gillard towards the endless rows of shelving. 'Because there's MORE to come. Another of Fair-Line's BIG, BUMPER SURPRISES!' (The horoscope, thought Mr Gillard wildly. That's what it had said in the *Bugle's* horoscope. He'd get a Fantastic Surprise if he crossed the Threshold of Fate!) 'The shopping spree . . .' the manager was saying, '. . . the shopping spree you have always dreamed of!' He consulted his watch as someone thrust a wire trolley into Mr Gillard's hands. 'You've got just two minutes to fill that trolley with Fair-Line goodies! Everything and anything you grab from the shelves! Now stand on that chalk-mark, and don't move until I give you a little prod in the back!'

(There it was again! The Influence of Jupiter, prodding him into action!)

'Your . . . your name isn't J-Jupiter, is it?' croaked Mr Gillard.

But his voice was lost in the uproar that filled the store. 'All set, old son?' the manager bellowed in his ear. 'You may never get another opportunity like this again! So GRAB it with both hands!'

Mr Gillard shook his head dazedly. His horoscope was coming true, right down to the very last word. He almost fell into the trolley as the manager bawled, 'On your mark! Starting count-down now! Five . . . four . . . three . . . two . . . one . . .'

'GO!' yelled the whole store.

At about the same time that Mr Gillard received a prod in the back, and went skidding towards the Frozen Foods Section, Mrs Goodenough was puttering slowly homewards on her Yamaha. Very slowly, in fact, because it was still a bit windy. And strong winds gave her a tendency to wobble.

And then there was that silly horoscope she had read in her staff copy of the *Bugle*. Mrs Goodenough, a Scorpio, wasn't particularly superstitious, but there was something about Englefield's new feature which had struck an odd, unnerving chord. A little shudder ran through her as the words of the horoscope seemed to slide across her goggles, in fiendish, glowing letters. 'YOUR LIFE IS ENTERING A MOST UNSETTLED PERIOD, AND YOU WILL DO WELL TO WEATHER THE STORM. IT MAY BE WISE TO CANCEL, OR POSTPONE A JOURNEY, BECAUSE YOUR SIGN SHOWS A DOWNWARD TREND. LOOK OUT FOR A DARK MAN WHO MAY CROSS YOUR PATH.'

Mrs Goodenough let out a little cry, as another gust of wind buffeted her crash-helmet. The wind seemed to be getting worse. Perhaps, she thought fearfully, it was bringing the 'storm' that she would do well to weather!

Now don't be silly, Hilda, she told herself. All that stuff about signs having a downward trend, and cancelling journeys, was just a lot of nonsense concocted by young Englefield. There was absolutely nothing in it at all. Even so, there was no harm in just ... *postponing* her journey home a little, at least until the wind had died down. If her memory served her right, there was a little coffee bar somewhere along this street, on the left hand side. A nice cup of coffee would help to calm her nerves. Make her forget about that ridiculous horoscope.

As Mrs Goodenough began to reduce speed, the wind swooped into the street again; a chaos of sound and fury. She heard a sudden, sharp 'KRAAK!', and then something whirled across the sky, and crashed into the road, right in Mrs Goodenough's path. There was no time to stop. There was a loud metallic crunch as Mrs Goodenough rode straight over the object, before braking to a stunned, trembling halt.

Gasping for breath, she pushed up her goggles, just as a man came rushing from the doorway of a nearby restaurant. A man who seemed to have leapt right out of young Englefield's horoscope! 'LOOK OUT FOR A DARK MAN WHO MAY CROSS YOUR PATH,' it

had warned. And here was by far the darkest man she had ever seen, bearing down on her! He was waving his arms, and uttering what to her sounded like a stream of horrifying threats and oaths.

It was too much for Mrs Goodenough. With a frantic cry of 'HELP! POLICE! KEEP HIM AWAY!' she executed the fastest kick-start of her life, and went blasting away down the street, narrowly missing the startled owner of the Taj Mahal Indian Restaurant.

Raising his arms in a baffled shrug, he addressed the little crowd which had gathered. 'Now why does she go tearing off like that? I am only wanting to apologise to the lady!'

'I expect she was suffering from shock, mate,' someone said. They all looked at the crumpled, white elephant, lying in the middle of the road. 'Your sign only missed her by a couple of feet! If she'd been going any faster, it would have landed right on her nut!'

For some reason he couldn't quite explain, Ed awoke the following morning thinking about Erica Roberts' hat-trick. If Erica's horoscope was as accurate as Karen had claimed, it must have got the other girls pretty excited. With a strange feeling that all might not yet be lost, Ed casually brought up the subject during breakfast.

'Of *course* they were excited!' Karen snapped. She was still sulking over Ed's lack of interest the previous evening. 'Especially when they found out that the Grovelands' goalkeeper's name was Brenda!'

'*Brenda?* What's that got to do with it, Karen?'

'The letter "B", you idiot! Erica's horoscope said that the letter "B" was significant!'

'Crikey!' said Ed. No wonder his sister had cycled all

the way home in her hockey boots. 'What happened then?'

'Well, they *all* wanted to read their horoscopes, of course ... in *my* copy of the *Bugle*. But I wouldn't let them!'

'Good for you, sis!'

'I told them to go out and BUY themselves a copy. But what was the point?' Karen pouted sarcastically. 'The Mighty Editor had given up, and gone home! You weren't even there!'

'*Cyril* was there!' said Ed, barely able to conceal his own excitement now. 'He took some copies of the *Bugle*, and said he was going to try and sell 'em round the sportsfield.'

'Ah, that REMINDS me!' Mrs Englefield broke in. She had been listening vaguely to the conversation, while trying to stop Baby Joe from dropping a chunk of his poached-egg sandwich into the waiting jaws of Charles the Fourth. 'Cyril popped round yesterday evening, Ed. I told him you were feeling a bit down, so he left a little message—'

'Message? What about, Mum?'

'I meant to tell you last night, when I brought up your supper. But I was so far behind with the housework, it went clean out of my mind, until now!'

'Mum, the MESSAGE! What did he *say*?'

'Something about the *Bugle*, I think. Yes, that's it! Cyril said to tell you that he'd sold *all* his copies of the *Bugle*. Every last one. And he'd got the money for them, too!'

'GLRRR-ROOOOO!' cheered Baby Joe, as he scored a direct hit on Charles' huge pink tongue. Mrs Englefield beamed at the delighted baby. 'Yes, darling, isn't it encouraging? I mean, Ed didn't expect his magazine to do so well, this month, did he?'

She looked round as a chair crashed over, and feet went thudding out into the hall. 'Ed? ED, where are you going? Come back here and finish your breakfast!'

But not even a double-portion of beefburger and spaghetti rings could have halted Ed. Within a few hectic minutes, he was cycling flat out for school, with Cyril panting at his side, gasping out confirmation of Mrs Englefield's amazing news.

'It must have been Erica Roberts' hat-trick that set 'em off,' Cyril blurted. 'Cor, it'd be funny if some of the other horoscopes have come true as well, wouldn't it, Ed?'

It would be fantastic, thought Ed. The miraculous boost that the *Bugle* needed! Why, there might be hundreds of excited girls waiting outside the door of his office at that very moment.

In actual fact, there were only seven girls, and a couple of second-year boys. But they were all chattering about Mr Gillard and Mrs Goodenough. And something that had happened to another girl from the hockey team. Apparently, she had gone to bingo with her mother, the previous evening, and won second prize in the raffle. Just as her horoscope had predicted. '*A small investment now,*' it had promised, '*will pay dividends later.*'

Ed couldn't sell *Bugles* fast enough! Even Ray Towler, who usually pinched a copy, drifted in. 'If it'll work for Erica Roberts, maybe it'll work for me in our next footer match!' he had sneered, for the benefit of his cronies. But from the way they hurried off with their *Bugle*, in a subdued, muttering group, Ed sensed that Towler was intrigued.

And so was Mr Forbes. It was well known that he had

a crush on Miss Townsend, one of the art teachers, but she had so far failed to respond to his advances. 'If your horoscope is anything to go by, Englefield,' Mr Forbes laughed nervously, 'I've a feeling that my luck is about to change! I mean, look what it did for Mrs Goodenough!' he went on. 'Her nerves are still shattered after that narrow escape, so she's taking the day off. But she sends you her gratitude, Englefield. She said if it wasn't for you, the elephant would have landed right on top of her! At least, I think she said something about an elephant . . .'

Ed hadn't the faintest what Mr Forbes was talking about. But he didn't really care. He had just experienced the dizzy, unbelievable delight of selling his very last copy of the *Bugle*, when Mr Gillard came breezing in.

'Here he is,' he cried. 'Edward Englefield – the literary genius of Baker Street School!' Ed had never seen the Assistant Headmaster in such a cheerful, bubbling mood. 'And how many copies of the *Bugle* have we sold THIS month, eh?'

Fifty, sir,' said Ed. The words seemed to thunder through his brain, like a tumultuous roar of applause. 'Every copy I printed. There's such a demand, I'm even thinking of printing some more.'

'I'm not in the least surprised, lad. As I said, that horoscope feature of yours was a stroke of genius.' Mr Gillard drew Ed aside, his voice dropping to an awed whisper. 'But how on earth did you *do* it, lad? I've never known anything so . . . so *uncanny*! All that stuff about crossing the threshold. I mean, I *hate* shopping in supermarkets!'

'My . . . er . . . mum isn't so keen on 'em either, sir,' said Ed, catching Cyril's eye. They exchanged a furtive, baffled shrug.

107

'But I certainly grabbed my opportunity with both hands,' the Assistant Head boomed on gleefully, rubbing his chubby palms together. 'Especially in the frozen food section. In the circumstances, Englefield, I shall be contacting your father, and asking him if I may present you with a suitable little reward for your efforts!'

'Er, thanks very much, sir,' said Ed. He'd really have to find out what had happened to Mr Gillard – *and* Mrs Goodenough. But at that moment, there was only one reward in the whole world that he wanted. And Mr Gillard seemed to read his thoughts.

'Of course, we couldn't THINK of closing down the *Bugle* now! Oh, dear me, no! I'll have all this sports equipment cleared out of your office this very day!' Mr Gillard strode across to Ed's battered duplicator. 'And to ensure that the school magazine maintains its present high standards, I might even treat you to another machine, out of my own pocket!' Tapping his lumpy nose, the Assistant Headmaster beamed, and winked at Ed. 'After all ... as you and I well know, Englefield ... I can *afford* it now, can't I?'

Ed just nodded, and beamed back. If Mr Gillard could afford it, that was his business. He was too limp with triumph to worry about teachers who had discovered a mysterious source of wealth ...

After school, as Ed and Cyril cycled slowly homewards, each of them devouring a large, toffee-flavoured ice lolly, Cyril said, 'D'you reckon it's true about Mr Forbes, Ed?'

'What's that, Northy?'

'There's a rumour going round that he's had a love-letter from Miss Townsend.'

'Good for him.'

'Wonder if it had anything to do with his horoscope?'

'Yeah, I wonder,' said Ed.

'But how DID you do it, Ed? I mean, how DID you know that all those fantastic things were going to happen?'

'I didn't, said Ed. 'I just copied the horoscopes out of one of our mum's magazines, and changed 'em round a bit.'

'You didn't?' gasped Cyril. Pulling over to the side of the road, he tugged out his own, crumpled copy of the *Bugle*. It had suddenly occurred to him that he hadn't even read his own horoscope yet. 'Let's see if it works for me,' he said eagerly. 'My mum says I'm a "bull"!'

'That's Taurus,' Ed told him. 'Well, go on, then. What does it say, Northy?'

His voice taut with anticipation, Cyril began,

109

'SATURN ENTERING YOUR BIRTH SIGN WILL BRING ENORMOUS, EMOTIONAL CHANGES. THIS WILL MEAN THE END OF SLEEPLESS NIGHTS, WORRYING ABOUT YOUR LOVED ONE. SO SHRUG OFF THOSE BLUES, AND LET RO-MANCE ENTER YOUR HEART. YOUR DEEPEST YEARNINGS ARE ABOUT TO BE FULFILLED!'

Cyril looked up, blinking in amazement. 'Well, *that* doesn't mean much, does it? I mean, it's all about love an' that. And I haven't even got a girl-friend.'

'I thought you fancied Sandra Tavener?'

'I do. But she's going out with Johnny Rackham now. So there's no point letting romance enter my heart, is there?'

'Guess not,' mused Ed. He must have forgotten to re-write the Taurus horoscope. 'What about mine, Northy?' I'm a "Capricorn". Read out what it says for Capricorns.'

'BEWARE OF MAKING AN ERROR OF JUDGE-MENT ,' Cyril intoned. 'WITH THEIR SIGNS BADLY ASPECTED, CAPRICORNS ARE ADVISED TO CONCENTRATE ON CON ... SOL-I-DATING THE PRESENT, RATHER THAN LOOKING TO THE FUTURE. A PROJECT YOU ARE WORKING ON SEEMS DOOMED TO FAILURE!'

Even Ed was amazed. 'That's *crazy*! I mean, its look-ing into the future — with the horoscopes — that saved the *Bugle*. And that's the "project" I was working on.'

'And it didn't fail, did it?' said Cyril. 'Fact is, Ed, this was probably one of the best days of your life!'

'*The* best,' said Ed.

They cycled on, thoughtfully consuming the last of the lollies.

'You know what, Ed?'

'What?'

'I never did believe in those horoscopes, anyway.'

'Me neither,' Ed said absently. His thoughts were already reaching into the future. Making plans.

'Hey, Northy. What's the name of that rock-group that's doing a concert at the town hall, next week?'

'You mean ... "Chocolate Teapot"?'

'That's it ... Chocolate thingey.'

'What about 'em, Ed?'

'Oh, I dunno, Cyril. I just thought ...' Ed paused, smiling to himself – savouring the thought of what he was going to say next. Especially *one* word in particular. 'I was just thinking of interviewing 'em for the NEXT issue of the *Bugle*.'

More Beaver Books

We hope you have enjoyed this Beaver Book. Here are some of the other titles:

The Beaver Book of Football A Beaver original. Useful advice on improving your game and buying and looking after equipment, as well as a brief history and some amazing facts about football. Written by Tom Tully and illustrated by Mike Jackson, with a Foreword by Phil Parkes

The Adventures of Nicholas and the Gang Whether they are having their photographs taken at school or playing cowboys and Indians in the garden Nicholas and his friends just can't keep out of trouble! A collection of hilarious stories by René Goscinny; illustrated by Sempé

Famous Lives: Sport A Beaver original. Football players, mountaineers, land speed record breakers, swimmers, motorcycle racers; this book is packed with fascinating information about 176 of the world's greatest sporting personalities. Devised by James Moore, written by Eric Inglefield and illustrated by Peter Dennis

Adventure of the Strange Ruby Pat and Tessa go to the rescue of their friends Faith and David, inheritors of a priceless ruby which is said to bring bad luck to its owners. Written by Enid Blyton and illustrated by David Barnett for readers of eight to twelve

These and many other Beavers are available from your local bookshop or newsagent, or can be ordered direct from: Hamlyn Paperback Cash Sales, PO Box 11, Falmouth, Cornwall TR10 9EN. Send a cheque or postal order, made payable to The Hamlyn Publishing Group, for the price of the book plus postage at the following rates:
UK: 30p for the first book, 15p for the second book, and 12p for each additional book ordered to a maximum charge of £1.29;
BFPO and EIRE: 30p for the first book; 15p for the second book plus 12p per copy for the next 7 books, thereafter 6p per book;
OVERSEAS: 50p for the first book and 15p for each extra book.
New Beavers are published every month and if you would like the *Beaver Bulletin*, which gives a complete list of books and prices, including new titles, send a large stamped addressed envelope to:

Beaver Bulletin
Hamlyn Paperbacks
Banda House
Cambridge Grove
Hammersmith
London W6 0LE

201201